WHERE MAGIC RULES

WHERE MAGIC RULES
A Cracked Mirror Press novella

ISBN: 978-0-9885599-7-4 (Print)
ISBN: 978-0-9831871-6-5 (Kindle)
ISBN: 978-0-9831871-6-5 (EPUB)

Where Magic Rules

Carmen Webster Buxton

Cracked Mirror Press
Rockville, MD

Other Cracked Mirror books by Carmen Webster Buxton:

The Sixth Discipline
No Safe Haven
Tribes
Shades of Empire
The Nostalgia Gambit
King of Trees
Saronna's Gift
Alien Bonds (coming soon)

For Risa, who proved
that a writer can be friends
with her copyeditor

ONE: A MYSTERY

"Good morning, sir."

Joe came awake with a jerk. He had been dreaming he was getting coffee at Starbucks, but the stone walls of his room told him he wasn't in Glencoe, Illinois. In this world there was no Starbucks, no Illinois—and no coffee.

The boy who waited by his bed looked about ten—skinny, with brown hair and gray eyes and that solemn air so many children had here.

"Good morning," Joe said, in passable Katoah. Not knowing the language when he first arrived had been frustrating—and dangerous. "Do I know you?"

"No, sir." The boy ducked his head. "My name is Mirek. Mother Wilhelmina would like to see you as soon as it's convenient."

Joe swung his feet to the floor and rubbed the stubble on his jaw. "Has there been another assault?"

"No, sir." The boy backed up and nodded at a tray on the dresser. "I brought you something to break your fast."

Joe saw a bowl of porridge, a slice of bread, and a cup of steaming brown liquid. Herb tea, one step up from dishwater. Joe recalled his dream. If only he had managed to drink the coffee before he woke! "Thanks," he said, getting to his feet. "Please tell Mother Wilhelmina I'll be there soon."

The boy bowed and left.

Joe washed quickly. Even with steaming hot water from the copper ewer on the pot-bellied stove, a sponge bath in a chilly room was no fun. The early morning sun that streamed over the shutters provided light but no heat. The shutters gave Joe some privacy, as his rooms looked out on the central courtyard, a mark of his favor with the Great Mage. He checked himself in the mirror and decided he couldn't put off shaving another day. He used a steel straight razor to scrape the whiskers from his face and remembered shaving in his apartment in

Glencoe, in the bright luminescence of electric lights, with hot water gushing from a tap, shaving cream foaming from a can, and a safety razor with disposable blades sliding painlessly across his face. He gave a mental sigh for what was lost to him.

Joe pulled on his clothes and wolfed down his breakfast, then cut through the central courtyard to reach the infirmary. The chill air still held vestiges of winter's icy grip. It had been a hard winter, but at least the cold had kept the dark lords at bay.

Joe's boots crunched on the gravel as he crossed the courtyard. Mother Wilhelmina wasn't in the tiny room that served as her office. Joe hesitated, then stepped back into the corridor. At the other end, a figure in a long gray robe and veil appeared.

Joe started toward her. "Mother Wilhelmina!"

She nodded but didn't increase her speed. She was far from elderly, but she was old enough for Joe to feel that the obligation to hurry was his.

He walked briskly until he was close enough to converse. "Good morning, Mother. You wanted to see me?"

Under her veil her plump face looked as serene as it always did. "Good morning, Joseph. Thank you for coming."

She had a faint accent; her Katoah sounded softer, less Germanic. And every time she said his name, Joe missed his home. He had been Joey when he was little, then Joe in school, but his mother had always called him Joseph. From the day he met her, Mother Wilhelmina had done the same. "Is anything wrong?" Joe asked.

She smiled reassurance, her brown eyes warming. "Not precisely. I wanted to ask you something."

"What is it?"

"Come this way." Mother Wilhelmina took his arm and led him down the corridor, pulling him into the ward for women patients. She walked to the end of the room where wicker screens enclosed a bed. Joe was surprised to see that the figure lying on the bed was a man, a boy actually. He had very short brown hair—Joe would have described him as having a crew-cut—and no sign of a beard. He lay on his back, his eyes closed, and didn't stir. His finely sculpted features gave his young face a great deal of resolution.

Joe recognized him at once. "So he made it?"

"This is the boy you rescued?" Mother Wilhelmina said.

Joe was surprised into staring at her. "Yes, of course. When I saw him fall, he looked so young, I hated to think he might die, even though I knew he was on the other side. Will he live?"

"Oh, yes."

Joe took a moment to glance over the screens at the rest of the ward. "What's he doing here? Is the men's ward full? I thought there weren't many casualties."

"There weren't. He's here because he's a she."

Joe gawked at her. "A she? You mean he's a girl?"

"A woman, actually," Mother Wilhelmina said. "Sister Gertruda estimates her age at about twenty-one or twenty-two."

Joe turned back to the figure on the bed, still incredulous.

"Is it so difficult to believe?" Mother Wilhelmina asked.

"Yes," Joe said. "I mean, he—she looks like a boy."

"But then, young boys are often difficult to distinguish from young girls."

"I suppose so." Joe stepped closer to the bed.

"What's wrong?" Mother Wilhelmina said. "You still look shocked."

Joe shrugged to convey his uncertainty. "I don't know. His—her hair is very short, but back home plenty of girls wore their hair short—although not usually this short. She could be a rock star—or a soldier in the army."

"She was a soldier in a dark lord's army," Mother Wilhelmina said, her tone dry. "I presume you mean the army in your homeland, the one that you were in when you came to us?"

"I wasn't a full-time soldier," Joe said. "I was in the Reserves—like an emergency army." He glanced down at the wounded woman again. "Why would she pretend to be a man?"

"I'm about to ask her. But first, I wanted to know if she was truly fighting in the battle."

Joe could recall the scene easily enough. "Yeah, she was really fighting. She took at least one of our men out. I don't think she killed him, but it wasn't from lack of trying. She had a sword, and she knew how to use it."

"Very well, then," Mother Wilhelmina said. "I'll proceed now."

She stepped to the table beside the bed and lifted a water glass, then took a vial from her pocket and measured four drops into the water. The water turned cloudy, and Mother Wilhelmina swirled it around. When she stepped to the bed, she didn't attempt to get the patient to drink the mixture, as Joe expected, but instead held the glass under her nose. After a moment, the woman on the bed stirred and jerked her head away.

"That's better," Mother Wilhelmina said. "Open your eyes, my dear, and speak with us."

The woman opened her eyes at once and tried to sit up, but the best she could manage was to prop herself up on her elbows. She had gray-green eyes, Joe noticed.

"Where am I?" she demanded, in perfect Katoah. "What place is this?"

"You're in the infirmary, my dear," Mother Wilhelmina said, her tone soothing. "You've been wounded, but you'll recover."

The woman looked groggy but alarmed. She glanced around wildly. "Whose infirmary?"

"Why, mine. My name is Mother Wilhelmina, and I serve the Great Mage."

The wounded woman looked shocked and struggled to sit up. "I'm a prisoner?"

"Now, now." Mother Wilhelmina stepped closer and put a hand on her shoulder. "You mustn't worry about that now. You need to rest."

"Rest?" the wounded woman said with scorn. "A plague on rest." She slid her feet to the floor and paused as if to gather her strength.

"Joseph, help me get her back into her bed," Mother Wilhelmina said.

Joe took a step closer, and for the first time the woman looked at him.

She stared at his face, and then opened her mouth in a scream of terror and rage. "No! Get back! Don't touch me!"

Nonplused, Joe hesitated where he stood.

"Wait, please, Joseph," Mother Wilhelmina said. "My dear, if you'll get back in bed by yourself, I won't have to ask Joseph to help you."

The woman wavered, and then moved to put her feet under the covers. She still stared at Joe, but her hands clutched the blankets.

When she twisted her torso, Joe saw she wore a necklace, a short chain with a small stone dangling from it. The white stone looked like an agate; a wire cage held it securely on the chain.

"What a curious bauble." Something in Mother Wilhelmina's voice told Joe that she was more than mildly interested. She stared at the necklace, and then shifted her gaze to the young woman's face. "What's your name, my dear?"

"Phillip," the woman said. "My name is Phillip."

Mother Wilhelmina smiled as she smoothed the covers. "Surely you realize that we've discovered your secret? Your name can't really be Phillip."

"Yes, it is!"

"But you're a woman, my dear," Mother Wilhelmina said gently.

"I'm not a woman!" the patient said, her voice rising in pitch. "I'm a man, and my name is Phillip!"

Mother Wilhelmina stroked her cheek. "Let's be reasonable, my chick. At least twice a day you must have to face the truth—and every twenty-eight days, you have a special reminder."

The woman called Phillip flushed and turned her head away. Mother Wilhelmina's hand darted forward and snatched the dangling stone. Holding it tightly, she pulled it as far away from the woman as the chain would allow.

"No!" Phillip screamed. "No! Give it back!"

When she began to beat Mother Wilhelmina with her fists, Joe jumped forward to restrain her. As soon as his hands grasped her shoulders, Phillip looked up at him and screamed again, a high keening wail of despair.

Before Joe could do anything else, Phillip sank back on the pillow in a dead faint.

"How very peculiar," Mother Wilhelmina said.

"I'll say," Joe said. "What the hell was that all about?"

"I don't know." Mother Wilhelmina had let go of the necklace. Now she reached over and picked up the agate. "Did you ever see a necklace like this one?"

Joe shrugged. "I don't think so."

Mother Wilhelmina slipped the chain through her fingers. "It's too short to pull over her head, and yet it has no clasp."

"Try to break it," Joe said. "It looks like gold, and gold is soft."

Neither he nor Mother Wilhelmina could break the links, however. Finally, Mother Wilhelmina again mixed a cloudy potion that she held under the woman's nose. This time Joe smelled the fumes and turned his head away.

Phillip gasped and sat up with a jerk, then screamed again when she saw Joe standing near her bed.

"Sheesh!" Joe said, retreating a few steps. "What's with her?"

"I don't know, but I intend to find out." Mother Wilhelmina took one step closer and slapped her still-screaming patient on the face. "Stop it!"

Phillip's mouth dropped open in indignation.

Mother Wilhelmina shook her finger and spoke severely. "Be quiet, young woman! You're disturbing our other patients."

"I'm not a woman!"

Mother Wilhelmina smiled grimly. "If you'll tell me why you're so afraid of Joseph, I'll send him away. Once we're alone, you can disrobe and we can discuss your gender at greater length."

Phillip flushed a deep red color. "I don't *know* why. I never saw him before. Make him go away."

Mother Wilhelmina nodded. "Very well. Go away, please, Joseph. Ask Sister Gertruda to send someone to assist me."

"Are you sure it's all right to leave you alone with her, Mother?"

"I'll be fine," Mother Wilhelmina said. "Go, please, Joseph, and do as I ask."

Joe looked appraisingly at the boyish figure, decided Phillip was too weak to pose any real threat, and headed for the door.

Behind him he heard Mother Wilhelmina speak. "Phillip, if that's what we're to call you, let's have a look at your wound and see what else we find."

Two: A Mage

Joe stepped out into the courtyard of the Great Mage's palace and looked around with a calculating glance, trying to see the place as he had the first time he had come to it.

Flagstone walkways crisscrossed a large grassy square surrounded by granite buildings. Only a few scraggly bushes softened the lines of the rough-dressed stones. Bounded by the main hall, the infirmary, the laundry, the cook house, and a guard room, the courtyard served both as a workplace and a thoroughfare. People routinely hauled wood and water, hung laundry, swept the flagstones, and tended livestock. Today a peddler had set up a stall, and a troubadour sang and played a lute, her cap artfully placed near her feet for passersby to fill with coins.

The troubadour wore mannish clothes—trousers, a knee-length tunic, and a loosely tied jerkin—but unlike the wounded warrior, she made no attempt to hide her femininity. The ample lines of her figure were obvious.

Joe thought back to the previous day, when he looked through the telescope at the fight raging on the other side of the barrier the Great Mage had erected. Joe had seen men fall and likely die; he had seen dreadful wounds inflicted by both sides. But only when he looked on the face of the seeming-boy had his heart been moved enough to risk the Great Mage's displeasure. He hadn't hesitated; he hadn't heeded the cries of the sisters who waited to tend the wounded. He had vaulted from the platform and had picked his way through the fray, evading the armed but exhausted men around him. He recalled how the woman's wound had bled freely when he found her, alarming him at the same time it reassured him she wasn't dead.

"Sir?"

Joe came alert with a start, aware that the same boy who had awakened him now stood deferentially in front of him. "It's Mirek, isn't it?"

"Yes, sir."

"You're new here, aren't you?"

"Indeed, sir. I came last week."

Possibly he was an orphan. The Great Mage's palace provided lodging and education to a good number of orphaned children, many of whom stayed to serve him as adults. "Did you want something from me?"

"Yes, sir. The Great Mage directs that you attend him at once."

The direct order gave Joe a twinge of apprehension. The Great Mage usually worded his requests more courteously. "I'll go now. Where is he?"

"In the solar, sir."

That didn't sound too bad. The Great Mage usually sat in the sunny room on the top floor of his palace for pleasant pastimes, rather than for business. Joe took the stairs two at a time. When he reached the top floor landing, he found a half dozen of the Great Mage's retainers waiting in the hallway.

"Oh," Joe said in confusion. "Is he busy?"

The Great Mage's steward stretched his lips in an ersatz smile. "He may well be busy, but he told us to admit you as soon as you arrived." He nodded at the two guards who held the door open for Joe. "I don't envy you the attention."

Joe wasn't certain himself as he stepped into the long, rectangular room. The dozen tall windows on the side walls had been glazed with small, diamond-shaped panes of glass. The many impurities in the glass made faint, fuzzy spots in the air.

"Come in, my friend, come in." The Great Mage stepped out of the shadows and into the sunlight. The first time he had heard that warm, confiding voice, so rich in timbre and inflection, Joe had felt a shiver up his spine. He still felt it, sometimes, and this was one.

"Good morning, sir." Joe advanced to bow politely.

The older man held out his hands. "Good morning, my friend Joe. Come closer. I would touch you."

Joe felt the shiver grow to a tremor of anxiety. People said the Great Mage's touch let him play a person's heart strings like a harp. Joe had never found the experience unpleasant; if anything, he always felt soothed afterwards. Still, like medicine that made you feel better, the mage's touch wasn't entirely welcome. "I'm fine, sir. I haven't had any more nightmares."

"And yet, yesterday you disobeyed me, Joseph. Isn't that true?"

"Yes, sir," Joe said, distressed to find himself sweating. The Great Mage seldom called him Joseph, and when he had, it had not been a good thing.

The Great Mage slipped his hands into his voluminous sleeves. He wore a simple gray robe, much like Mother Wilhelmina's. His short, crisp beard had gone white, and his hair had thinned to nothingness in a spot on the back of his head, but he was only ten years older than she was. "Do you remember what I said when I gave you leave to stand on the platform during battles?"

The Great Mage was half a head shorter than he was, but Joe felt somehow as if he were looking up. "Yes, sir. You told me I could take the telescope and watch the fighting so long as I stayed on this side of the Barrier."

"Precisely! And yet you thought that you had license to jump the wall?"

"I didn't mean to disobey. It was just—"

The Great Mage waited, but Joe was unable to articulate his reasons.

"Well?" the mage demanded.

"It was just that the boy—I mean the woman—looked so young and vulnerable. The thought that he—she—might die seemed too horrible to contemplate. I didn't do it consciously. I just couldn't stop myself."

The Great Mage's expression stayed impassive for a moment, and then he gestured to a low-backed chair. "Sit, Joseph."

Joe sat down. It took an effort of will to stay seated and let the mage come up behind him. When the older man put his hands on Joe's shoulders, he couldn't stop himself from jerking in reflex.

"Relax!" the Great Mage said.

A feeling of calm well being crept over Joe. He took a deep breath and let it out with a sigh of relief.

"That's better," the mage said, his hands still warm on Joe's shoulders. "Now tell me about this woman who looks like a boy."

Joe related the story of watching the fight, of vaulting the wall and retrieving the fallen enemy soldier. He rambled on about the twisted, bloody rings in the soldier's mail shirt, and the way her red blood had pooled on the green grass.

"Very good," the Great Mage said when he finally finished. "Now tell me about your dream last night."

Joe thought back to the moment he had awoken, groggy from sorting out the old reality of his dream from the new reality of this world. An image flashed in his mind. He had ordered a large black coffee, but the young woman who handed it to him from behind the counter had had delicate, pale yellow wings. Not so real after all.

He hadn't said anything aloud but the Great Mage spoke anyway, amusement in his voice. "The woman who gave you this beverage you crave had wings?"

"Yes, sir. Very pretty wings. Rather like a moth."

"Ah! And do you know of any people in our world who have wings?"

"No, sir." No, there were no fairies or elves here. Mages and dragons, yes—although he had never seen a dragon—but no fairies or elves.

The mage's voice held warm concern. "Then why do you think you dreamed of a person with wings?"

"I don't know exactly. I suppose she represented magic, and there's no other way I can explain what happens in this universe except to say that here, magic rules science."

"I suppose that's as good a way as any of putting it." The mage lifted one hand from Joe's shoulder and placed it on his forehead.

Joe felt an incredible heat, as if he suddenly had a fever.

"Do you remember what I said about the difference between myself and the dark lords?" the Great Mage said.

"That you're a benevolent despot. You said you're all despots, but there's nothing benevolent about them."

"Remember it, Joseph. I will not tolerate disobedience."

Joe held his breath, but the mage's hand slipped from his forehead to rest briefly on his shoulder, and he sensed a return of favor.

"Now," the mage said, sliding his hands back into his sleeves, "I think I had best see this young woman warrior myself. You will accompany me, Joe."

"Must I, sir?" Joe asked, rising to his feet. "She screams every time she sees me."

"Does she, indeed?" The mage smiled as if he found this amusing. "We shall see."

⍵

The woman did scream. She took one look at Joe and let out a fierce cry of rage. Sister Gertruda had to restrain her.

"I told you, sir," Joe said. "May I leave?"

"Certainly not," the mage said. "Stop that, young woman."

"Please, sir," Sister Gertruda said. "Call her Phillip. She won't answer to anything else."

"Be quiet, Phillip!" the Great Mage ordered. "Be quiet, or I shall cast a spell on you!"

Phillip shut her mouth and stared at the Great Mage in alarm, then scrambled to the far side of the bed. "Who are you?"

"I think you know who I am." The Great Mage looked her up and down and frowned. "I begin to suspect that I know you, also."

"My name is Phillip!"

The mage's eyes lit in an amused smile. "Phillip it shall be. How are you today, Phillip?"

She didn't answer right away. She looked at each of them in turn. "I'm well enough." Her tone sounded both reluctant and wary.

The Great Mage nodded. "I'm pleased to hear it."

"Her wound wasn't deep, my lord," Sister Gertruda said, "and it's healing well."

"Am I a prisoner?" Phillip asked.

The Great Mage's smile became inscrutable. "Have you been treated badly?"

"No." Again there was reluctance in her voice.

"We don't often take prisoners," the Great Mage said. "Usually your lord's soldiers test the strength of my magic by assaulting the Barrier. We retaliate, and they retreat, slaying those of their wounded who cannot walk. My friend Joe has truly saved your life."

Phillip looked across the room at Joe, but he couldn't see any gratitude in her glance. She didn't speak.

"Now," the Great Mage said with brisk efficiency, "Where did you get your necklace, Phillip?"

She flushed and lifted her chin. "I've always had it."

"Ah!" The Great Mage moved closer to the bed and scrutinized her intently.

She returned his stare, not flinching even when he stepped closer. "You don't frighten me, old man."

"Don't I?" Suddenly the mage lunged forward and grabbed her by the arm.

Phillip gave a strangled gasp but didn't otherwise cry out. It looked to Joe as if she wanted to pull away but couldn't. Joe could identify with that feeling.

"Joe!" the mage said. "Take the stone in your right hand. Pull it as far away from Phillip as you can without hurting her."

Joe obeyed reluctantly. He folded his right hand into a fist around the stone, then pulled the chain to its full length, which was not very far.

The Great Mage took a step closer and shifted his grip to Phillip's shoulders. She gave a little sigh, a faint, breathy whisper, and closed her eyes.

The three of them stayed frozen for almost a full minute. Joe was wondering if Phillip had fallen asleep when she opened her eyes and looked at him.

She seemed to Joe to be staring at him hungrily, as if he were something she wanted very badly.

"Now," the Great Mage said, "let go of the stone, Joe, and step back a pace."

Joe obeyed. As soon as the stone again lay on her skin, Phillip's angry glare returned. She said nothing, however, until the Great Mage released her and stepped back.

"Keep that man away from me!" She shouted at the mage, but she pointed at Joe. "Keep him away, or I'll kill him!"

Her fierceness stunned Joe. She sounded sincere.

"You have a poor sense of gratitude," the Great Mage said. "Joe saved your life."

Phillip grimaced and gave Joe a sulky scowl. "Thank you. Now go away."

"Fine with me," Joe said. "May I leave now, sir?"

"Not just yet," the Great Mage said. "I've finally determined why you came to us, Joseph."

Joe blinked in surprise. "Sir?"

"I said when you accepted me as your overlord that I would keep you close until the day I found enlightenment about your purpose here. Do you remember?"

For the past three years Joe had wondered if that day would ever arrive. "Yes, sir."

The Great Mage's expression grew serene. "Your purpose is to help Phillip find her true self. You'll have to start right away."

Joe's jaw dropped, and at the same time, Phillip blurted out an angry expletive.

"Now, now," the Great Mage said. "Such language isn't appreciated here, Phillip. You'll have to learn to guard your tongue."

Sister Gertruda fluttered near the bed like a moth near a candle. "My lord, she must keep quiet! The wound could reopen if she doesn't."

"Precisely," the Great Mage said. "I think a small sleeping draught is in order, sister."

"A curse on you and all your progeny!" Phillip shouted. "May they all sicken and die terrible deaths!"

"I have no progeny," the Great Mage said, unperturbed. "No child of my body, in any event."

"Then may the worms eat you, as you lie cold and forgotten in the earth!"

"The worms eat everyone who dies," the mage said. "No one lives forever, and no one is remembered forever. Your curse applies to everyone, sooner or later."

"Then I shall make it sooner!" Phillip cried, lunging at the Great Mage.

Joe jumped to intercept her. Holding her back without hurting her proved a difficult task.

Sister Gertruda entered the fray with a cup of sleeping draught, but it was only when the Great Mage took hold of Phillip's arm that she became calm enough for Sister Gertruda to hold the cup to her mouth.

The wounded woman choked and swallowed, then dashed the cup to the floor. "Take your bloody swill elsewhere, you pig of a woman!"

"How much did you manage to give her, sister?" the mage asked.

"Enough," Sister Gertruda said with grim satisfaction. "She'll sleep soon."

"Bastard!" Phillip pulled free from Joe's slackened grasp and sank down upon the bed. "For all your high-sounding phrases, you're no better than a dark lord."

Sister Gertruda gasped in indignation. "Mind your tongue!"

Phillip looked as if she would like to retort, but instead, she merely lay down as if she were exhausted.

"The sleeping draught is working," Sister Gertruda said, pleased.

"Yes," the Great Mage said, as Phillip closed her eyes. "As soon as she's sound asleep, have her conveyed to Joe's room."

"My room?" Joe blurted out. "Why?"

"Because you're going to tend her while she heals," the Great Mage said. "You need to get to know each other better before you leave on your quest."

"What quest?" Joe said, feeling as if the floor had rocked under his feet.

The Great Mage shrugged. "I haven't decided yet."

THREE: A QUEST

Joe set his shoulders and nodded at the guard who stood outside his door. The man looked impassive as he held the door open, but Joe suspected he would grin at the other guard after he had closed the door behind Joe.

The screaming started as soon as Joe stepped into his room.

"Get out, you bloody bastard! May the plague take you and all your kin!"

Joe set the tray down on the dresser. Phillip made no move toward him, but Joe knew that was only because she was manacled to his bed by the short chain on her ankle.

He kept out of her reach and sat down on the cot he had slept on since the day that a sleeping Phillip had been carried into his room. "I don't like this any better than you do, but neither of us has any choice. The Great Mage gave me orders to take care of you, and I have to follow them. Would it hurt to shut up and eat your dinner?"

She glared at him but said nothing.

"That's fine," Joe said, encouraged. "You don't have to talk. If I pass you your dinner, will you eat it and not throw it at me?"

This time the glare was more restrained. She had enlivened breakfast with a flight of crockery in his direction. Angry at having to clean up the mess, Joe had declined to bring her any food at noon, so he knew she must be hungry now.

"Very well," she said.

In the three days he had cared for her, Phillip had cursed him, struck him, and shouted at him, but she had never lied to him. He removed his own dinner from the tray, placed the tray on the floor, and pushed it toward her with one foot.

Phillip retrieved it as soon as it came within reach. She sat on the edge of the bed and ate hungrily, but with a cautious air, never taking her eyes off Joe.

19

On the other hand, she didn't shout at him. "That's better, isn't it?" he said. "Surely you don't want to live like this?"

"Of course not." She rattled the chain on her ankle. "No one wants to be a prisoner."

"I don't mean that. I mean the screaming and shouting. Why do you hate me so much? You don't act like that with anyone else."

"I don't know." She made the admission grudgingly, as if she disliked the fact that she couldn't account for her own actions.

"You don't remember me from the fight, do you?"

"You weren't in the battle." She said it flatly. Hardly surprising since she had been unconscious by the time he had picked her up.

"I wasn't in the fighting, but I saw you fall. I ran to fetch you."

"Why were you watching?"

Joe shrugged. "I trained many of our soldiers. The Great Mage won't let me fight with them, but I feel a need to be there."

Finally, this piqued her curiosity. "You train soldiers, but you're not a soldier?"

"I was once, but not in this world."

Her eyes grew wide at this. "Not in this world?"

Joe nodded. "In the universe I was born into, the world is a very different place. The moon is the same here, and I can find familiar patterns in the stars, but the land and the people are different."

Phillip looked baffled. "How are people different here?"

"Well," Joe said, "in my world, there's no magic, but people make things using science."

Fairly hooked, Phillip tucked her feet under her as she sat on the bed, the chain on her ankle rattling noisily. "What things?"

Joe related a little about what life was like in the United States of America in the early twenty-first century.

Phillip tilted her head and managed to look both amazed and skeptical. "But, if there's no magic, what makes the machines go that carry you so quickly?"

"Their engines make their wheels turn. The engines burn fuel called gasoline."

"Where do you get gasoline?"

"Out of the ground."

"Pish!" she said. "You can't burn dirt."

"It's not dirt."

She still looked skeptical. "How did you get here? Are there more people like you here?"

"Not that I've met, although the Great Mage said there were some in the past." Joe leaned forward and rested his elbows on his knees. "I came through entirely by accident. I was on an Army exercise when—"

"So you were a soldier?" Phillip interrupted.

Joe decided not to try to explain the concept of part-time military service. "Not all the time, just every so often."

Phillip wrinkled her nose. "But how did you get here?"

"I don't really know." Had it been his destiny to come here or merely the bad luck to be in the wrong place at the wrong time? If he hadn't needed the ROTC scholarship in college, he wouldn't have been in the Reserves. "I was on a training exercise. We were waiting for orders when I saw this peculiar glow a little ways up the hill from me—bright and hazy, like a fire except there was no smoke.

"I walked closer, and I heard a scream, like someone was hurt, so I ran. When I came over the hill, a sort of golden haze enveloped me like a fog. I tried to run back, but somehow I wasn't in a meadow in Illinois anymore.

"There was this house, and it was burning. A woman was screaming. A man was holding her down on the ground while another man looked like he was going to rape her. I shouted at them to stop, and they looked up and saw me."

Joe paused as the memory overwhelmed him.

Phillip waited a moment and then prompted him. "What happened?"

Joe shrugged. "They looked as surprised as I felt. They said something that sounded like cursing, but I didn't understand it.

"Two more men ran out of the house, and one of them came at me with a sword. I managed to avoid him, but someone hit me from behind. The next thing I knew, I woke up in a dungeon in Lord Elsen's palace."

She said nothing at this, but her gaze narrowed and Joe thought she looked faintly suspicious.

"I was chained, and there were rats everywhere," he went on. "They had taken all my clothes and left me with a big lump on my head, but no food and no water. After a while, three men came in. One was a guard, one was there to ask questions, and one was a torturer.

"He was a good torturer," Joe said, his tone grim as he recalled the details, "but I didn't understand a word any of them said. I would have told them anything if I could have made them understand me, but I couldn't. So eventually, I passed out.

"When I woke up, they gave me some water and started again. After three days of that they threw a few rags on me, hauled me out of the dungeon, and took me to Lord Elsen."

Phillip stirred on the bed. "How did you know it was Lord Elsen?"

"I didn't—not then. He was in his great hall when they dragged me in front of him. He had my belongings spread out on a table—my uniform, cell phone, radio, and gun."

She looked perplexed at this part of the narration. Joe had used English words, as Katoah had no comparable words for the products of technology. "Cell phone? Radio? Gun?"

Joe nodded. "Cell phones and radios are for talking to people when you're far away from them. A gun is a weapon that kills from a distance—sort of like a bow, but more deadly. Since I wasn't on a live-fire exercise, though, it wasn't real ammuniition. The gun couldn't actually hurt anyone."

"Oh."

"Anyway, Lord Elsen looked me over as if I were a specimen brought out for his amusement, which I suppose I was. One of the guards made me kneel while his lordship looked me over. It was then that I knew I was in a truly different world."

Phillip tucked her knees under her chin. "Did Lord Elsen do magic?"

"Yeah," Joe said, "he did some tricks. He squeezed his hand into a fist, and suddenly I couldn't breathe. He was choking me without touching me.

"When he opened his hand, I got my breath back. Next he took a white-hot poker out of the fire and held it in his bare hands. I thought it was an illusion until he used it to set the ropes that bound me on fire. The guards laughed before they put the fire out. And then Lord Elsen put his hand on my shoulder, and I was in agony. I pleaded with him to make it stop. When he finally did, though, he kept his hand on my shoulder and said something stern.

"I told him I didn't understand, and I think he could tell what I was saying, if not the actual words. Then one of the guards brought over my gun and my radio and shoved them in my face.

"Lord Elsen shook my shoulder and glared at me. I guessed that he wanted to know what the things were for. I mimed speaking into the phone and the radio, and firing the gun. He was most interested in the gun.

"I pulled the trigger, but it wouldn't fire at all. I didn't know then that magic was real here. I didn't understand that it could make something not work.

"He had them take me to a room in the servants' quarters. They kept me locked up, but they fed me, gave me clothes and medicine for the burns. And every day a man came and taught me Katoah. I found out Lord Elsen's name then, and when he had me brought to him one day, to see what I was learning, I found out why he was keeping me prisoner."

"Why was he?" Phillip sounded genuinely interested.

"He wanted to know more about how the gun and the other things worked. He was thinking that if he used magic together with science, he could make weapons no one else had."

Phillip's eyes flickered. "So how did you get here?"

"I planned an escape. Every time they took me outside for exercise, I noted the placement of doors and windows. Then one day a guard was careless. I managed to steal a tin fork and made a lock pick from it. I opened the door to my room in the middle of the night, and whacked the sleeping guard with the water pitcher."

Her eyes opened wide with reluctant admiration. "Did you kill him?"

"I didn't stay around to find out. I had a couple of close calls—I had to kill a sentry—but I made it out. I ran all that night and all the next day with very little rest. Luckily for me, I finally came to the Great Barrier."

"What did you do?"

"I walked along it for about half a day but I was having trouble staying on my feet because I hadn't had any food or water in days. I had just started across an open stretch of ground when a mounted party broke from some trees and headed straight for me. I recognized Lord Elsen's livery, and I tried to run, but I fell. I was lying there in the dirt when a raiding party came out from behind the Barrier and set upon my attackers. They drove them off, and then they took me before the Great Mage."

"Your benefactor?" Her tone implied skepticism.

"Yes. By then I could make myself understood. When the Great Mage moved close and put his hand on my shoulder, I thought I'd be tortured again, but it wasn't like that. If anything, he made me feel well."

"Mages are all alike," Phillip said bitterly. "Those who work magic prey upon the rest of us, who have no power to resist them."

It seemed a harsh philosophy considering her circumstances. "And yet you served a dark lord?"

She shrugged. "A masterless dog is a stray, free to starve and be whipped by all who see him."

"So you feel no loyalty to Lord Marcellin?"

"I was raised in his ward. I was working on a farm when a squad came through looking for men. I didn't try to get away. Better a demon you know than one who's new to you—and better him than Lord Elsen."

Joe was wondering how to ask her if Lord Marcellin's officers had known she was a woman without setting off a vituperative reply when Phillip asked him a question.

"What about you? If you're truly from this strange other world, why do you owe loyalty to the old mage?"

"When he first met me," Joe said, "he told me that when people came through from my world, they were stuck here. And then he explained to me how all the land for hundreds of miles is governed by half a dozen mages, each holding ward over his or her land. He told me I was free to go if I liked, but that if I stayed in his ward, I'd have to swear an oath of loyalty and obedience to him. When I decided to stay, I had to kneel in front of him, put my hands in his, and swear to be loyal and obey him."

"And have you done so?"

"Yes," Joe said, "until the day I saw a boy lying wounded and in danger of bleeding to death. I forgot my orders then, and went to bring him to safety."

Phillip said nothing for a moment, and then she hunched one shoulder in a defensive gesture. "I said thank you."

"I heard you. I also heard you threaten to kill me. Why would you want to kill me?"

"I don't know! I don't know anything except I have to keep away from you!"

Joe grinned humorlessly. "The Great Mage has made that rather difficult."

Before she could answer, the door swung open. Joe jumped to his feet, well aware that there was only one person who would enter his room without knocking.

"Good evening," the Great Mage glanced from the tray on the bed to Joe's dinner dishes on the dresser and smiled. "It's nice to see the two of you sharing a meal so amicably."

"Let me out of here!" Phillip said. "You have no right to make me stay here with him!"

"Don't I?" the Great Mage asked.

"No!" she shouted back. She waved a hand at Joe. "He's been telling me how Lord Elsen kept him prisoner. What makes you any better?"

"Have you been tortured or deprived in any way?"

"No."

"And has Joe offered you any insult or subjected you to any indignity?"

"No."

"Well, then, it seems I'm at least slightly better than Lord Elsen."

She ground her teeth and looked around her as if she were searching for a weapon.

"Phillip!" the Great Mage said sharply. "Would you like to wear this?" He signaled the servant behind him, and the woman held up a pale blue, low-cut gown adorned with lace.

Phillip looked utterly revolted. "Take it away. I don't want it."

"If you don't behave," the mage said, "I'll have the sisters remove your clothes, and you'll have to wear this dress or go naked."

She said nothing.

"There will be no more shouting or cursing at Joe," the Great Mage said. "There will be no more crockery thrown—or anything else."

She still said nothing.

"I won't ask for an oath," the mage went on. "Time enough for that when you're ready to leave on your quest."

"Quest?" she said. "I'm going on a quest?"

"Oh, not alone," the mage said. "Joe is going with you."

"Bloody hell!" Joe said.

The Great Mage smiled but didn't comment.

"Why should I go on a quest for you?" Phillip demanded. "I owe you nothing, old man."

"I know you feel no loyalty toward me," the mage said. "But I also know you'll keep an oath if you give it. If you complete this quest with Joe, then I'll let you go free once it's done."

"What quest?" Joe demanded. "Where are we going and why?"

The Great Mage managed to look both solemn and amused. "To the mountains in the west. I need to make a potion that requires a half dozen dragon's scales. You're going to fetch them for me."

Four: A Dragon

Joe hefted his pack onto his back and shifted its weight to get the best balance. The weight of the sword and its sheath still felt unfamiliar. Beside him the woman known as Phillip also hefted her pack, but unlike Joe, her only weapon was the knife on her belt. The Great Mage hadn't wanted to arm her too thoroughly.

"Ready?" Joe asked.

She nodded, and the two of them set off again, heading westward into the setting sun.

Joe glanced at her as they trudged along. She insisted on walking several yards away from him, but at least she kept up well. Mother Wilhelmina had assured him her wound was healed enough for her to travel.

Joe still had difficulty in seeing Phillip as a woman, even after more than three weeks in her company. The image he saw in his mind refused to mesh with what he saw with his eyes. Even now, if he shut his eyes and thought about her, he almost expected to see a different person when he opened them.

Back in the real world, a girl he had known in high school had surprised everyone by moving to California and then returning six years later as a man. And Joe was pretty sure one of the women he had known at work had started life as a man. But those people had seemed well adapted; they had resolved the issue, and it showed. With Phillip, there seemed to be a constant mental war going on. Joe wished he knew who all the combatants were. Somehow, Phillip seemed to think he was one of them.

Joe sighed and studied the landscape of rolling hills. They had been hiking all day. The morning of the day before, Philip had sworn to the Great Mage that she would help Joe acquire six dragon's scales and not harm him along the way. The mage had provided supplies, a map, and a mounted escort as far as the Great Barrier.

They had left the Barrier fort at the western-most gate that morning, along with the soldiers of their escort. Joe had been sorry to leave them, but Phillip had scoffed at his caution, agreeing with the mage that, if one was to go on a quest, one went alone and on foot.

"May I see the map, please?" Joe asked after they had walked some distance further.

Phillip stopped, shrugged off her pack, and then pulled the leather map case from it. She handed the cylinder to Joe.

"Let's see where we are," he said, unrolling the large vellum sheet. The map showed the entire valley in detail. A thin red line marked their route, due west from the palace. The line cut through the oddly-shaped oval representing the magic-reinforced wall known as the Great Barrier. From the gate, the line headed straight for the mountains. They would have to be careful; straying too far south would cause them to wander into Lady Merida's ward. It took the likes of Lord Elsen to make the Dark Lady seem a reasonable neighbor.

Lord Elsen's ward was, thankfully, well to the north. Lord Marcellin's ward lay to the east, beyond the Great Barrier—little chance of straying there by mistake.

The necessity of traveling together required acknowledgement of each other's need for privacy. Back at the palace, Joe had left the room and summoned a servant when Phillip needed to use the chamber pot. Here, whichever of them felt a need simply wandered off for a few minutes.

On their second day of hiking, they entered the foothills of the mountains. The ground sloped upward steeply, and walking took more effort. Fir trees grew thickly on either side of the trail; their fragrance reminded Joe of Christmas.

Late in the afternoon, they came to a village in a clearing. The man who came out to greet them looked wary, but the sight of the Great Mage's seal on their map case must have put his mind at rest, as they were welcomed.

A farmer gave them a hot supper, a welcome meal after three days of trail rations. Over a bowl of mutton stew, Joe asked about dragons.

"Oh, no," the farmer's wife said. "We don't get dragons here abouts. You have to go higher into the mountains. They nest in caves."

"I hear there's one that lives on Dindale Peak," the farmer volunteered. "They say the Dindalers feed it sheep to keep it away from their children."

"They should have killed it long ago," his wife said. "Nasty, fierce things, dragons."

"Now, now," the man said in soothing tones. "You know as how the Great Mage doesn't hold with killing dragons."

The woman sniffed. "Well enough to sit in his lowland palace and say not to kill them. Us who live nearer the threat feel differently."

The farmer changed the subject, and Joe didn't mention dragons again.

They slept in the farmer's barn. In the morning, Joe and Phillip turned their steps toward Dindale Peak.

The slope grew steep, and the going got slower, but the trail was well marked and easy to follow. They stopped to rest more frequently. At mid-morning, they came to a wide, flat place on the trail.

"Why don't you rest here a moment?" Joe said. "I'll be back in a minute."

Phillip slipped off her pack and sat down on a boulder with an exhalation of relief while Joe walked off to find some privacy.

After thoroughly watering a pine tree, he had headed back through the underbrush when he heard an angry shout and a scream of pain. He broke into a run, but slowed as he came in sight of the boulder.

Two men held Phillip pinned against the rock. A third man facing them held his right hand to his own left arm. Blood seeped through his fingers. All three men wore ragged, dirty tunics and worn breeches. Clearly they weren't soldiers.

"You little bastard!" the third man said.

Joe ducked behind a tree and slipped off his pack as he peered around to watch what was happening.

The wounded man hit Phillip hard with a backhanded blow to her face. "Make sure he doesn't have any more knives," he ordered, knotting a rag around his arm.

The shorter of the two men frisked Phillip briskly, and then uttered a harsh bark of laughter. "He's not a boy; he's a girl!"

"What?" the wounded man said.

"He's a girl!" The short man patted Phillip's crotch. "There's nothing, Max. No balls, and no dick."

Phillip tried to pull away, but the taller man held her firmly. He was a very large man, with a scraggly beard, even more unkempt than his companions.

"Take his clothes off," Max said. "Let's see what we've got."

Joe debated the best way to attack. All three men were armed; the one called Max held his sword in his hand, while the tall man had sheathed his, and the shorter one had dropped his weapon onto the ground.

Joe pulled his sword as silently as he could, but he knew he wasn't a good swordsman. On the other hand, he had the benefit of surprise and his own skills. He started to maneuver closer.

The short man had slit Phillip's shirt and ripped it off, revealing her half-healed wound and a long strip of cloth wound tightly around her breasts.

"Ho, ho, you're right, Ulric! Our fresh-faced lad is a woman." Max's voice rose gleefully. "And she has a pretty trinket we can keep as a souvenir."

"I get her first!" Ulric said. "Last time Gavin nearly killed the woman before I got my turn."

"Don't be so impatient," Max said. "Let's look her over."

He pulled his knife. Joe prepared to rush in from where he was, but all Max did was slit the bindings, leaving Phillip naked from the waist up.

She had small breasts, but they were round and firm, and there was no denying her womanhood. Joe flitted behind a tree. He was close, but none of the three seemed to have noticed him.

Phillip was cursing her captors with a stream of obscenities that would have made some soldiers blush.

Max merely grinned in appreciation. "She'll put up a good fight. I think I'll go first."

If Ulric was going to protest, he lost the chance when Joe thrust the point of his sword into the outlaw's back and out his abdomen, before the man could utter a word.

Joe had never used a sword in anger; he was unprepared when Ulric dropped like a stone and the sword slipped from Joe's hand. Joe stood empty handed as the two startled outlaws turned toward him.

Max bellowed an angry curse and rushed to attack. Joe scrambled out of his way. Gavin let go of Phillip to draw his sword, which proved a fatal mistake, as Phillip quickly snatched up Ulric's blade and ran Gavin through from behind, much as Joe had done to the weapon's owner, except she kept her grip.

Joe was too busy trying to keep out of Max's reach to pay attention to her. Only when Phillip shouted at him did he realize she was holding two swords.

"Catch!" She tossed him Gavin's weapon and then immediately charged Max.

The outlaw turned on her with ferocity, but Phillip held her own, parrying Max's thrusts with a good deal more skill than Joe displayed when he joined in. After a few close calls, Phillip renewed her attack and forced the enraged outlaw on the defensive.

In the end, Joe served merely to draw the outlaw's attention and leave him vulnerable to Phillip' thrust. She sliced into Max's chest as he turned to deflect Joe's enthusiastic if inexpert blows.

The outlaw fell to the ground and gasped a curse. Phillip kicked his sword from his hand, leaned over him, and slit his throat in one motion. She straightened up, breathing hard and sweating, and gave Joe an angry glare. "You trained soldiers?" Her tone made it clear she considered this an unlikely happenstance.

"Yes," Joe said, "but not with swords. My specialty is unarmed combat." He bent over Ulric to make certain the man was dead, and then did the same to Gavin.

"An unappealing lot," Phillip said. "You took your time in getting back."

"Just as well. I took them unawares."

"A good thing for you," Phillip said tartly.

Joe realized he was staring at her. She looked like an Amazon warrior standing there bare-breasted, her blood-spattered shirt in tatters. Her eyes held a wild gleam, and her hand gripped Ulric's bloody sword.

Joe looked away hastily. "There's an extra shirt in my pack if you need it."

"I have my other one," she said, striding over to her own pack.

"I'll just get my things," Joe said, and he headed back to retrieve his pack. He took his time, and called out from behind a tree before he approached.

"Phillip? Can I come back now?"

She answered affirmatively, and Joe walked back down the trail to find her buttoning her spare shirt. He didn't see the one the outlaws had torn off of her, and he concluded she must have used it to bind her breasts. The attempt wasn't entirely successful, as the bulky shirt made her look more buxom rather than less.

Joe turned his attention to the dead outlaws. They had carried one large pack between them, but it had nothing of value in it except half a loaf of bread, a sack of turnips, and a pair of silver candlesticks.

"They were truly outlaws," Joe said. "Thieves as well as rapists."

"Very likely," Phillip said. "They wear no lord's livery and yet they went armed."

"The question is," Joe said, looking over at the bodies, "what do we do with them now?"

"Leave them. They wouldn't have taken any trouble for us."

It sounded callous. "Maybe not," Joe said. "But if we leave the corpses here to rot, it'll draw scavengers. It would be tragic if anyone were hurt or killed because they stumbled across a pack of wolves in a feeding frenzy."

Phillip didn't look persuaded, but Joe couldn't tell if she didn't believe such an event was likely, or if she didn't consider the possibility a tragedy. "We have no tools to dig graves,"

"Let's get them off the trail at least," Joe said.

In the end, they stripped all three bodies of their weapons and dragged them into the woods. When Joe saw that the hillside dropped precipitously into a gully, he directed Philip to help him tip the bodies over the edge.

As soon as the third body had slid down the hillside, Phillip trudged back to the wide place in the trail and began inspecting the dead men's swords. After hefting each and trying the balance, she settled on Max's blade as the best.

"You do very well with a sword," Joe said. "It doesn't come naturally to me."

Phillip looked faintly contemptuous. "Soldiers must be very soft in your world."

The disparagement in her tone stung him. "Don't be so quick to judge. You don't have much to go on."

Her smile radiated confidence. "I could take you easily."

The smile irked Joe as much as her words. "Are you certain enough to try a fight my way?"

"Your way?"

He nodded. "No knives, no swords, no weapons of any kind."

"You mean a fist fight?" She didn't look worried as she shed her new sword belt.

"I didn't say a fist fight. I only said no weapons."

"What other kind of unarmed combat is there?"

"It's called karate," Joe said as he shed his own belt.

"I never heard of karate." Phillip pronounced the unfamiliar word carefully.

"Are you afraid to try it?"

"No! With a weapon or without, I'm not afraid of you."

They faced off where the trail was widest. Phillip took the offensive, but Joe evaded all her efforts to strike him.

"You're fast," she said in irritation, "but you'll never win that way."

Joe smiled, turned as if he were going to move to his left, and then whirled around and leaped in the air at the same time, coming down in a fast axe kick that hit Phillip right in the stomach.

"Oof!" she said, doubling over.

Joe backed off. "Are you okay?"

"What's okay?" she gasped. "I don't surrender, if that's your question."

"It just means all right," Joe said. "I forget sometimes and use English words. You sure you want to keep going?"

"Yes!" she said, lunging at him suddenly.

Joe spun out of the way and caught her by the arm as she rushed past, flipping her over his hip and onto the ground.

Phillip scrambled to her feet and let out a stream of invective that ended in a wish for Joe to die a terrible death.

"Hush, now," Joe said. "Save your breath."

She attacked several times, but Joe always managed to kick or throw her without incurring any damage himself.

"Give up?" he asked as Phillip struggled to her feet.

"No!" She lunged again.

After he threw her to the ground, Joe jumped on her back and held her down with her arms pinned behind her. "Now do you give up?"

"Rot in hell, bastard!"

He sat up straighter. Every time she tried to twist or turn to dislodge him, Joe would tighten his grip and pull her arms back farther.

When Phillip screamed in pain, Joe relented.

"Why don't you just give up?" he said. "I'll admit you could skewer me in no time if we were fighting with swords."

She gave a convulsive shudder as she tried to move, and then went limp. "All right, I give up."

He stood up and offered a hand. She ignored it and got to her feet on her own.

"We'd better get moving," Joe said.

Phillip resumed her weapons and other possessions, and they started off in silence.

"What do you suppose they were doing in these hills?" Joe said after a while. "There can't be much loot for the likes of them."

She shrugged. "People think dragons hoard treasure. I don't believe it myself, but some people do."

"Do you know much about dragons?"

She shook her head. "Only what everyone knows. They fly. They breathe fire. They nest in caves. Sometimes they eat people. How about you?"

"The Great Mage refused to answer any of my questions, so I know less than everyone knows."

For the first time since they had stopped to rest, Phillip smiled in genuine amusement. "You'll learn more very soon, then."

Joe smiled back. "It looks like it, doesn't it?"

ω

Joe consulted the map after they ate a meal at noon. He concluded that they were very near Dindale Peak. "It looks a little like the picture, don't you think?"

Phillip studied the map, and then shrugged. "They all look alike to me."

Joe had to agree. "We need someone we can ask directions of—someone local."

Phillip glanced around. Except for a few birds and squirrels, nothing moved in the landscape. "There's no one about."

"We'll just keep going," Joe said, replacing the map in its case.

A short while later, a flock of black goats scrambled down the side of the mountain. A large scruffy dog brought up the rear, and a little ways behind him an elderly, gray-haired man leaned on a stick.

"There we go!" Joe said, cheerfully. "Good day to you, sir!"

The goatherd didn't seem pleased to be addressed by strangers, but he answered civilly. When told of their quest, he looked derisive. "Dragons is nonsense. I doesn't hold with dragons."

"You mean you don't believe they exist?" Joe asked.

"O` course they exist," the goatherd said. "Hard to deny when I seen one flying about, plain as day, a many a time."

"How do we find it?" Phillip asked. "Is it vicious?"

"Find it?" the old man said. "Stay round about long enough, and the old bastard'll find you, most like."

"You mean it eats people?" Joe asked.

"Not no more," the goatherd said. "Leastaways not since them Dindalers took to feeding it regular."

"Where do we find it?" Phillip repeated.

The goatherd had to be coaxed, but finally he revealed that the dragon had built a nest in a cave some distance up the side of the mountain. The cave could be reached by following a trail that branched off from this one; the turning could be distinguished by round stones piled into a pyramid.

"A marker it be," the goatherd added, "for the last young woman what he ate some time ago."

"Will the dragon be in the cave now?" Joe asked.

"Sure enough," the goatherd said. "He be a crafty old devil, but he likes his nap in the afternoon."

Joe found this somehow heartening. They thanked the old man and started up the trail.

They found the stone pyramid, and then the path up to the cave, less well traveled than the main trail, but visible.

They had a steep climb, scrambling up the side of the mountain using bushes and roots to pull themselves up. After half an hour the sight of a cave rewarded their efforts. The path led straight to it, and the grass around the entrance was flattened down.

"This looks like it," Joe said.

"Yes." Phillip didn't sound eager.

"You don't have to go in with me," Joe said. "You helped me get here. That's enough."

She gave him a contemptuous glare. "Don't be ridiculous. You'll never make it without me."

"Okay, then, what do you think is the best approach?"

She chewed her lip. "If he's really old, he may be willing to be sensible and let us take the scales. Otherwise, we'll have to kill him."

"The Great Mage doesn't like it when people kill dragons."

"Then he shouldn't have sent us here to get scales from one," Phillip said. "I'm going in. I'll stay as far to the right as I can. You go left. Try to stay hidden as long as possible. If we're lucky, maybe we'll catch him sleeping."

She started for the cave, and Joe followed a little behind her. He wished he could believe they would be lucky.

The wide cave mouth faced west, so the afternoon sun lighted much of the interior. Joe walked slowly, taking his time and studying the place. Phillip flitted silently to the far wall. When she ducked behind a large boulder, Joe could only see the top of her head.

The cave was mostly open space, with rocks and boulders strewn about on the floor, and stray bones scattered among them. Joe hoped the bones weren't human. The only signs of human habitation—clay pots and what looked like stone tools—suggested people hadn't lived in the cave for a very long time.

There was nothing that looked like treasure. Almost the only thing that wasn't rock was an enormous chest-high mound of leaves and branches near the back wall.

When the leaves rustled, Joe's heart pounded. The mound was the dragon's nest, and the dragon was at home!

$\mathcal{F}$IVE: $\mathcal{A}$ LESSON

Joe approached cautiously. The dragon lay curled up in serpentine loops, one on top of another, like a neatly coiled pile of rope that had slid out of shape. Its snake-like appearance surprised Joe. Its tail was pointed like a snake's, and its head, though large for its body, was wedge-shaped. Its scales were much less dense than a snake's, more like roof tiles than skin. Each iridescent scale gleamed in the faint sunlight, reminding Joe of sheets of mica.

Unlike dragons in the picture books of his childhood, this dragon's body never thickened, not anywhere on its great length. It had six limbs, four that resembled an animal's legs and two that looked more like human arms. All its limbs were muscular, but seemed insignificant when compared to its length. Nicks and scars covered both its bat-like leathery wings, as if they had seen hard use.

The dragon stretched one enormous wing out and licked the skin like a cat grooming itself. It rooted with its snout, as if it were looking for rough spots that needed to be smoothed down. Once it tugged at a clump of something until it pulled it free.

After its wings were clean, it folded them neatly across its back, gave a large, awesome sigh, and wriggled down into its nest. It reached down with its mouth and took a small black rock from a pile beside the nest. Tipping its head back, it let the rock drop into its mouth. Crunching contentedly, it lifted its head high. When it lowered its neck, its head came to rest on a large boulder, about ten feet from where Joe crouched.

"Greetings," the dragon said. "I didn't see you there at first—not until the wind shifted, and I smelled a human."

It took Joe a moment to realize that there had been no sound. The dragon hadn't made any noise, let alone spoken. The words had simply popped into Joe's head, in a voice that seemed indubitably masculine.

41

"It's a pretty nifty trick, isn't it?" the dragon reflected, still without speaking a word. "And you're an outsider, so you're not easily impressed."

Joe felt his skin crawl as he wondered frantically what to do.

"What can I do for you?" the dragon asked. "Got any villages that need exterminating?"

The mental tone was almost hopeful. In spite of his fear, Joe began to be amused. "Not at the moment."

"Too bad." The dragon gave another large sigh. "Who's your friend?"

"My friend?"

"The other human over there." The dragon flicked his large, curling eyelashes at the other side of the cave. "It smells like a woman, but she's difficult to read."

Joe grinned in appreciation of this sentiment. "Might as well come out, Phil."

Phillip stood up and stepped out from behind a large boulder, her new sword held at the ready.

The dragon studied her with interest. "Well, now, you *are* a surprise."

"I can hear you in my head!" Phillip cried, dropping her sword to clutch her ears.

The dragon was amused. "Of course. How else would a magic being converse?"

"Are you saying you can do magic?" Joe asked.

"Certainly." The dragon stretched his neck out so his head was very close to Phillip. "I expect she can, too. She has the power."

Joe was taken aback. "What power?"

"The power to do magic. All dragons are born with it, but only a few humans." The dragon gave Joe a condescending gaze. "You can't learn magic unless it's in you from the start."

Joe swallowed nervously. "Are you saying she's a mage?"

"Not yet. She doesn't know anything. But she could learn."

"Stop talking about me!" Phillip took a step closer, her sword forgotten. "You know nothing about me!"

The dragon blinked once and flicked his long forked tongue. "I can tell a lot about people just from looking at them, especially women."

"Why women?" Joe asked. This dragon was nothing like he had expected.

"Well, I've had more experience with women," the dragon explained reasonably. "I used to have human—er, visitors. You can learn a lot from women when they're, um, interested."

For a moment Joe thought he was talking about eating human prey, and then an even more revolting meaning hit him. "You're making that up!"

The dragon flapped his folded wings, as if to shrug. "Dragons don't lie. You can ask her."

"It's true." Phillip sounded dazed. "They don't lie."

"You really—you and a woman—" Joe couldn't bring himself to say the words out loud.

"Dear me, yes! They used to come, two or three every night and wait their turn. It didn't give me much of a thrill, but it was something to do. The only nearby female dragon isn't interested in an old crock like me."

His self pity was evident. Joe felt curiosity overcome his revulsion. "Are you expecting anyone this evening?"

"Oh, no." The dragon's self pity grew stronger. "They won't come near me now—not after I killed that girl. I tried to explain to the other one who was waiting, but she just ran down the mountain screaming bloody murder. Quite rude, I thought."

"How did you kill her?" Phillip asked.

The dragon got a reminiscent look in his eye. "It was simple carelessness. I'd begun to undulate and dance to excite her, just like I always did." The dragon began to weave his coils back and forth in a slow, sinuous, dancing motion. "Just as things got interesting, she happened to clutch a crucial spot just under—that is, a very intimate spot for a dragon. I quite lost my head, and I coiled myself tightly around her, crushing her rib cage like an eggshell. People got upset, especially when they found out that I'd eaten her."

"You ate her?" Joe said, horrified.

"Well, really, what's the difference?" The dragon was plainly miffed. "She was dead. That's what meat is—dead things. And I'm always hungry after—that is, I was especially hungry that night."

The urge to laugh overwhelmed Joe, even while he wondered how long it had been since the dragon had eaten.

The dragon didn't wait for him to ask out loud. "Just this afternoon. I had a very tasty sheep. The villagers leave them for me twice a week, regular as clockwork. It's part of the truce."

"What truce?"

"We worked things out," the dragon confided. "They calmed down. If you lie down with a dragon, you have to know there's a chance you'll get crushed and eaten. She knew the risks."

"So you don't raid villages anymore?" Joe asked.

"Oh, no. Too tiring, at my age." The dragon had been studying Phillip, and he suddenly darted his head back and forth in front of her. "My dear, what is that you're wearing? I haven't felt an enchantment that strong in decades!"

Phillip stepped back a pace and snatched up her sword. "I don't know what you're talking about."

The dragon closed his eyes and swayed his head back and forth. "Oooh, a masculinity spell. Lovely! Just what a feeble old dragon like me could really use!"

Phillip put one hand over her necklace and stepped back even further, gripping her sword tightly.

The dragon looked far from feeble. Indeed, he seemed quite excited as he darted his head back and forth from Joe to Phillip. Joe gripped his own sword in alarm.

"Oh, now," the dragon lamented, "you mustn't be afraid of me. I'm quite tired of people being afraid of me. There aren't that many of us left, and when we're gone, you'll be sorry. We're all that's holding the other world at bay."

"What do you mean?" Joe asked.

"Your world." The dragon dropped his head on a boulder as if he were too tired to hold it up any longer. "In your world there are no dragons and no magic, only science, right?"

Joe nodded.

"So you see how it works? Our magic can hold back science. You humans can't build those awful weapons I see in your mind."

Joe was stunned. Could the presence of dragons be the reason the laws of physics held no sway in this world?

"But you won't die," Phillip said. "Dragons live forever."

The dragon gave her a scornful look. "Nonsense! Nothing lives forever. I'm several hundred years old, but I shan't last another century."

"You don't look that old," Joe said.

"Thank you. But I am old."

"Can you still fly?" Phillip asked.

"Of course." The dragon's dignity was plainly wounded by this aspersion. "I can even do this."

He turned his head and gave a sort of belch. A five-foot flame shot out of his mouth and nearly singed Phillip's hair. She jumped backwards in alarm.

The dragon seemed pleased with her reaction. "You see?"

"We see," Joe said. "How do you do that? Is it purely magic?"

"Oh, no." The dragon shook his head, and faint puffs of smoke came from his nostrils. "I must be very lonely to tell you my secrets. To breathe fire, I have to eat fire stones."

He nodded at the pile of black rocks near his nest, and Joe saw that they were chunks of coal. "You eat coal?"

"Is that your word for it?" the dragon asked. "Yes, I eat it. It's tasty when you're in the mood for something crunchy to round out a meal."

"I can see where it would be." For a moment Joe wondered if he could be dreaming.

"This is all very interesting," Phillip said, "but it's getting us nowhere."

"Very true," the dragon agreed. "You must have come here for something. What was it?"

"We're on a quest," Joe said. "The Great Mage wants some dragon scales."

"The Great Mage?" The dragon pondered the name. "Oh, yes, I remember. His real name is Tolliver. Lord Tolliver they called him when he first came into his powers. Not a nice young man, but then few dark lords are."

The aspersion shocked Joe. "The Great Mage isn't a dark lord."

"Not now," the dragon agreed. "But when he was young, he could be as nasty as the rest of them."

"Yes, well, he's older now," Joe said. "And he needs six scales from a dragon."

The dragon opened his eyes wide. "Six! That old dog! He could make anyone fall in love with him with that much love potion."

"Love potion?" Phillip asked.

"Why, yes. That's about all our scales are good for. While they're on the dragon, they're hard as armor, but once they fall off, they crumble to powder in a week or so."

"What the Great Mage intends doesn't matter," Phillip said. "I made an oath to bring him dragon scales, and I will do so."

The dragon blinked and drew his head back. "Don't get your knickers in a twist, my dear. The nest is full of scales, and you're welcome to take them away." He moved, rolling his coils one after another until his entire body lay on the floor of the cave.

Phillip advanced and peered into the nest. She and Joe rooted through the leaves and found five intact scales.

"Only got five?" The dragon sighed, the first real sound he had made in a while. "Well, that's easily mended." He lifted a six-foot length of his body and rubbed it against the wall of the cave. Two scales clanged as they hit the stone floor. "There you go. One to spare."

"Thank you," Joe said. "You've been very kind."

"You're welcome. It was nice to have company. So long as people don't expect me to exert myself, I can be as polite as the next dragon."

Joe wrapped the dragon scales carefully in parchment and put them in his pack.

"Goodbye." Phillip moved toward the mouth of the cave as if she were eager to be gone.

"Are you saying goodbye already?" The dragon seemed reluctant to let her go. "Are you sure you wouldn't like to stay, my dear? Your friend could take the scales back to the mage while you, um, rest here with me?"

"No, thank you." Phillip flushed fiercely.

"Come along, Phil," Joe said, hefting his pack.

"Do come to see me again!" the dragon called as he settled back into his nest. "Drop in any time."

Six: A Conundrum

The day after the dragon gave them his scales, Joe and Phillip reached the foothills without incident. The next night they camped on farmlands at the boundary of the Great Mage's ward.

Joe's mood was cheerful as he built their fire. They had accomplished the task the Great Mage had set and hadn't had to kill the dragon.

"The Great Mage will let you go free now," he said to Phillip over dinner.

"Yes." She didn't seem interested.

"What will you do?" Joe asked.

"What?"

"Where will you go? Back to Lord Marcellin's ward?"

"I don't know."

"Do you have a family?"

A crease formed in her forehead, as if answering his question cost her mental effort. "I was an orphan. A farm family took me in when I was eight."

"I'm sorry," Joe said. He might never see his parents and his siblings again, but at least he had lost them as an adult and not a child of eight. "It must have been rough to grow up without a family."

Phillip didn't answer.

"Is anything wrong?" Joe asked.

Phillip tossed a twig into the fire. "I never said thank you."

"What?" Joe said.

"You saved my life when those scum were going to rape me. I never said thank you."

Joe felt compelled to point out the obvious. "Mostly you saved yourself."

She shook her head. "I couldn't have done anything if you hadn't come back. Thank you."

Joe stared at her for a moment, and then blurted out the question he had wanted to ask for days. "Why do you want to be a man so badly? I mean," he went on in a rush, trying to explain before she exploded in anger, "I can see why you might pretend to be a man. If you wanted to be a soldier, you'd have to pretend to be a man. But you seem to really want to *be* a man."

When she didn't say anything right away, he spoke hesitantly. "It's not a matter of—of sexuality, is it?"

She gave him a hard stare. "What do you mean?"

He held up a hand. "Don't get so hostile. In my world, there are plenty of people who feel attracted to their own gender. A few of them even feel they were born in the wrong body—the wrong sex."

Her eyes lit with eagerness. "Really?"

He nodded. "Sure. There are men who want to be women and women who want to be men." He waved a hand. "With the right surgery, they can get it straightened out. Sometimes they even fall in love, get married, and adopt some kids."

She blinked. "You mean that a woman could become a man and then marry another woman?"

"Sure. Why not?"

She grimaced. "I have no interest in women."

The comment left Joe at a loss. "Well, if you don't want to truly be a man, then why do you insist on acting like one?"

"I don't know," she said, despair in her voice.

"Maybe the dragon is right, and it's the necklace?" Joe said. "The Great Mage could help you take it off."

"No!" Despair had morphed into anger. "Don't you dare suggest that to him, or I'll kill you!"

Joe stared at her in surprise. "Sheesh! You're really something."

Phillip looked abashed. "I'm sorry, okay?" she said, enunciating the word carefully.

Joe was surprised into a laugh. "Hey, that was pretty good."

She smiled at him, and Joe thought she had never looked more appealing. After they had cleaned up from their meal he watched the way the flickering firelight made her face look almost delicate. After a while, he let his mind drift onto other thoughts as he stared into the fire.

"What are you thinking?" Phillip said.

"I don't think I should say," Joe said.

"Why not?" she said, curious. "Is it something bad?"

"I don't think so. You might not agree."

"What is it? Tell me!"

"Well," Joe said, "I was remembering that blue gown the Great Mage had—the one he threatened to make you wear."

"Why would you think about that?" she asked, amusement in her voice.

"I was wondering how you'd look in it. I had decided you'd look pretty damn spectacular."

She sat up. "I don't wear dresses."

"I know."

"You think because you saved my life a couple of times you can make me do things I don't want to do?"

"No."

"Because I won't! I won't be a woman for you!"

Joe sat up beside her. "I know that. Unfortunately, I can't stop thinking of you as a woman. I've tried, but I can't."

"So what do you expect me to do about it?"

"Nothing. It's not your problem. You don't need to worry about it."

She turned her back to him. "I thought you were someone I could trust."

The pain in her voice alarmed him. "You can trust me."

"No, you're like Lord Marcellin's soldiers. All men are interested in is forcing women to rut with them."

Having his feelings lumped in with the impersonal lust of nameless mercenaries made Joe mad as hell. "Just because the men in Lord Marcellin's guard have no respect for women doesn't mean every man is that way. I never a touched a woman unless she wanted me to touch her. And people don't rut, they make love—if they care about each other."

Phillip spoke with her back to him, her voice muffled. "So you've—you've made love to lots of women?"

"I wouldn't say lots."

"How many?" she asked, still with her back to him.

"I don't know," he said, mystified. "Does it matter?"

"I was just—just wondering if there's been anyone since you came to the Great Mage's palace."

Still confused, Joe hedged. "Three years is a long time."

"So there is someone?"

"What's going on here?" Joe knit his brows in a tight frown. "I told you I can't stop thinking of you as a woman, and you jumped on me for that. Somehow we're now tallying up my sex life. If I didn't know better, I'd say you were jealous. Why are you acting this way?"

Finally she turned around to face him. "I'm not acting any differently."

"Like crap." Joe frowned. Her eyes had welled up, and her face looked red and splotchy. "You look as if you're about to cry."

"I never cry."

"Maybe not, but you're damn close to it now."

She turned her head away, and Joe put one hand gently on her shoulder. "What's wrong, Phil?"

As soon as he touched her, he felt her body stiffen. She gasped, and all at once she seemed to have difficulty in catching her breath.

"Are you okay?" Joe asked in alarm.

"Oh yes! It's so different now!"

"What?"

"Don't let go," she said throwing her arms around him as she twisted to face him. "Whatever happens, don't let go of me!"

"I won't." Joe folded her into an embrace to offer comfort and was surprised when she lifted her face and kissed him. "Damn," he said when the kiss ended. "I never saw that coming. What are you up to, Phil?"

She pulled his shirt open and ran one hand over his torso. "Don't let go of me, and everything will be fine."

Stunned, Joe grabbed her hand. "You want to make love? Right here?"

"What's wrong with right here?"

"Nothing," Joe said, throwing his scruples to the winds. "So long as you're okay with this, right here is just fine."

"You talk too much," she said, and she pulled his head down to kiss him again.

ω

Joe woke to find himself lying on his back with Phillip sleeping on her side, her head cradled on his chest. Joe looked down at her and wondered how he could ever have thought she was a man. Her slenderness gave her a kind of angular beauty that the dawn's soft light made very feminine. Phillip stirred and opened her eyes.

Joe smiled at her. "Good morning."

She seemed confused and pulled away from him as she sat up, naked except for her necklace.

"Anything wrong?" Joe asked.

Phillip jerked once, as if she had received an electric shock, then started to shake. She hunched over.

Joe sat up next to her. "Are you okay, Phil?"

"Get away from me!"

It was said with her old fierceness. "What's wrong? Are you sick?"

"Just get away!"

Joe blinked, flabbergasted. The night before, Phil had been as tender a lover as he had ever had. "After last night you want to go back to 'don't come near me or I'll kill you'?"

She jumped up and stumbled away from him. "Last night—nothing happened last night."

"Nothing happened? That's right up there with you're not really a woman."

She sat down on a fallen log and began to rock back and forth. "I can't be a woman! I just can't!"

"Why not?"

"I don't know."

Joe gave up. He sat down on the blankets, picked up his trousers, and began to pull them on. "I've had it. We take the damn dragon scales to the Great Mage, and after that, it's fine with me if I never see you again."

Phillip retrieved her clothes and dressed without saying a word.

They walked in silence for most of the morning. Joe tried to talk, but Phillip wouldn't respond.

Finally, Joe decided it would be better to clear the air. "Look, Phil," he said as they trudged along, "I know it was your first time, and I apologize if I said or did anything that made it difficult for you."

She didn't answer. Joe had despaired of a response when she gave him a hard stare and asked a question.

"Did you mean it?"

"Did I mean what?" Joe said.

"Did you mean it when you said it would be fine with you if you never saw me again?"

Would he care if he never saw her again? She might be incredibly difficult to deal with, but she had somehow gotten under his skin—more under his skin than anyone ever had, here or in the real world. "No, I didn't mean it. I don't know why, but I'll miss you when you go."

This seemed to be enough of an answer. Phillip began to comment on the sights they passed—a river that meandered southward, interesting rock formations in the now distant peaks, the decreasing frequency of trees in the landscape, and such concrete signs of civilization as cart tracks.

She seemed so relaxed that Joe was taken aback when she stopped suddenly and uttered a curse word.

"What's wrong now?" he said.

"I don't know." Her eyes scanned the countryside as if she were convinced there was something there she wasn't seeing. "But something—something is watching us."

Joe didn't discount her fears. The dragon had said she could work magic. "What is it?"

"I don't think it's an it," she said. "I think it's a them."

"Then who are they?"

She shook her head, then shivered. "I don't know, but they're not good."

Joe glanced around but saw nothing. "I'm perfectly willing to run like hell on your say so. But which way?"

Phillip pointed. "To the river!"

She started running, and he followed. The two of them ran flat out, leaping into the air like a pair of startled hares as they jumped a small creek.

Just as Joe wondered if Phil could be wrong, he heard the thunder of many hooves pounding the ground. A quick glance over his shoulder made his heart freeze. The riders wore Lord Elsen's livery.

"Faster!" He let his pack fall from his shoulders.

Phillip let her pack drop and the two of them ran full tilt toward the river.

All at once something seemed to drag down Joe's limbs. He could barely lift his feet. "Keep running!" he shouted as he fell to the ground. "Run, Phil, run!"

She gave him a quick, anxious look, and then glanced back at their pursuers.

"Run!" Joe managed to gasp, as even speaking became too difficult. He lay on the tall grass and watched her sprint madly away, heading south toward the river. He lay with his head on the ground, and the noise of horses' hooves became a pounding roar.

Just before the dust rose and obscured his view, he saw Phillip pause on the river bank. She drew her sword and held it up, then jumped feet first into the river.

Suddenly milling horses surrounded Joe, their hooves so close he feared being trampled. The horses calmed as their riders dismounted. Booted feet approached.

A familiar voice spoke over Joe's head. "The other one may prove more interesting, but this one has value."

Joe still couldn't move, not even when Lord Elsen leaned over him.

"You remember me, eh? That's good. You'll know that I don't make idle threats."

Joe didn't even try to speak.

Lord Elsen frowned. "Surely you have something to say for yourself? Or has the cat got your tongue?"

A sudden pain stabbed Joe's tongue. He screamed as blood ran from his mouth.

"Ah!" Lord Elsen said. "You, at least, have no innate magic. This will be easy enough."

Joe groaned, and focused his will on trying to break the grip of Lord Elsen's magic. He managed to raise his upper body a foot or so off the ground.

"You prefer to do things the old fashioned way?" the dark lord screamed at Joe. "Here's your first lesson!"

Lord Elsen's booted foot lashed out at Joe's head, and then darkness swallowed him up.

Seven: Pain

Joe returned to consciousness, aware only of pain. His head ached; his tongue throbbed; the muscles in his arms and legs were in agony.

When he opened his eyes he saw that he was moving across the same open plain. His limbs pained him because he was tied spread-eagled to a crudely-built rectangular wooden frame; he bounced along, suspended by his wrists and ankles, one extremity bound in each corner as a horse pulled the frame over the ground. Joe felt every jolt whenever a support hit a rock or a hole.

It had only been mid-morning when he and Phillip had started to run, and now the sinking sun told him it was late in the day and they were heading north, toward Lord Elsen's ward.

Just at that moment, Lord Elsen appeared in Joe's field of vision, riding a large black horse that trotted easily beside Joe's prison frame.

"Ah, good," Lord Elsen said, smiling, "you're awake."

Joe said nothing.

"We'll stop soon," Lord Elsen said, "There are a number of things you need to tell me."

"I have nothing to tell you." It distressed Joe to hear the words come out as a harsh croak.

"We shall see." Lord Elsen glanced over at the sun and then back at Joe. "Very soon now, we shall see." He kicked his heels into his horse's sides, and the animal broke into a canter and carried Lord Elsen out of Joe's view.

Joe wasn't sorry to see him go, but he now had nothing to distract him. The muscles in his arms and legs pained him terribly, and his mouth was dry because he was thirsty—very thirsty. He tried counting the number of men to take his mind off his thirst, but he could only see the sixteen who rode behind the horse that pulled him along.

A short while later, the caravan halted. Four men unhooked the wooden frame from the horse. They lifted the frame upright, and two of them held it in place while the other two fetched small shovels and dug two holes in the earth. All four of them lifted the frame and placed the ends of the vertical sides into the holes. Once it was in place, they filled the holes in and tamped down the dirt.

When they finished, the frame stood upright, and Joe hung suspended by his wrists. It brought some relief to the muscles in his legs, but increased the pain in his arms.

"Wait!" Joe called, when the men started to walk off. "Could I have some water, please?"

Only one man even looked back, and he merely shook his head.

The other men built fires, laid out bed rolls, and began to prepare food. Joe fell to wondering if Phillip had found safety. She no longer had the map or any supplies, but she had her sword. Joe suddenly realized he didn't know if Phillip could swim, and he felt a grim fear that she might have drowned. He shut his eyes in desolation, and when he opened them again, Lord Elsen stood right in front of him.

"Good evening," Lord Elsen said politely.

"Go to hell," Joe croaked.

Lord Elsen's smile wasn't pleasant. "Eventually, perhaps, but not just now. In the meantime, I have some questions for you."

Joe shut his mouth tightly, and Lord Elsen stepped closer.

"How did you get out of your room?" Lord Elsen said.

Joe was so surprised at the question, he answered it. "I picked the lock."

"With what?"

"A fork."

"Ah," Lord Elsen said. "You're a resourceful man."

Joe said nothing.

"My spies tell me you found favor with the old mage," Lord Elsen said. "What did you teach him of your world?"

Again, Joe said nothing.

"Who was that with you when we caught you?"

Joe maintained his silence.

Lord Elsen moved closer. "I shall have to test your resolution." He pointed with his index finger, and everywhere he pointed, that part of Joe's body radiated intense pain.

The suddenness of it made Joe scream. The pain moved up and down his torso as Lord Elsen moved his hand, and then stopped as abruptly as it had started.

"Answer my questions!" Lord Elsen said. "What did you teach the old mage?"

Joe gritted his teeth and said nothing.

Lord Elsen stepped close, pulled his knife, and held it to Joe's throat.

Joe closed his eyes and swallowed hard. He heard Lord Elsen laugh, and then felt the knife's edge move down his torso. When he opened his eyes, Lord Elsen had slit open his shirt.

The dark lord laid the blade of his knife flat against Joe's bare chest. After a moment, the blade grew hot. In seconds, it was hot enough to make Joe try to pull away.

Lord Elsen pressed the knife even tighter against Joe's skin. The blade began to glow red.

Joe screamed as the knife seared his skin. He smelled his own flesh burning, and a thin plume of smoke rose in front of his eyes. When Lord Elsen finally moved the knife, a perfectly shaped impression of it had been burned into Joe's chest.

"Now," Lord Elsen said, "what did you teach the old mage?"

Panting, Joe tried to will himself to ignore the pain. He clenched his eyes shut, but found himself compelled to open them when hands gripped his shoulders.

Lord Elsen's face was only inches from Joe's. "What did you teach the old mage?"

Pure pain surged through Joe's body. He screamed again and again, until finally the dark lord moved his hands and the agony stopped.

"What did you teach the old mage?"

Joe hung limply in his bonds. When Lord Elsen lifted his hands again, Joe moaned. "No," he said feebly. "Please, no."

"What did you teach the old mage?" Lord Elsen said. "Tell me, or I'll do it again!"

"Karate," Joe croaked.

"What?" Lord Elsen said.

"It's called karate," Joe said. "I need water."

Lord Elsen called for water and held the bottle to Joe's lips long enough for him to drink a few sips. Then he pulled it away. "Tell me about karate! What is it?"

"It's a form of unarmed combat," Joe said, his voice stronger. "You use your hands and feet as weapons."

"The old man learned to do this?"

"Not personally. I taught his soldiers."

"And what else?"

"I showed his people how to make things."

"What kind of things?"

"Stoves," Joe croaked. "I showed them how to use stoves instead of fireplaces to heat a room. And how to use pulleys to lift things, and windmills to grind grain and pump water."

Lord Elsen looked impatient. "What about your weapons?"

"He wasn't interested in weapons."

Lord Elsen put both hands on Joe's shoulders again. Joe flinched, but there was no pain.

Lord Elsen clenched his hands so that his fingers dug into Joe's flesh. "Now tell me about the man who was with you when we found you."

Joe said nothing.

"He ran away and left you to your fate," Lord Elsen said, his tone coaxing. "He had the power to withstand what you cannot, and yet he left you."

Joe let his head drop back. He closed his eyes and waited for the pain to start.

Lord Elsen didn't disappoint him. Waves of pain coursed through Joe's body. Joe writhed in agony, but clenched his teeth and didn't say a word.

Finally, Lord Elsen stopped the pain but left his hands in place on Joe's shoulders.

"Now," the dark lord said, "think about this man. How do you know him?"

Joe tried to keep his mind blank but there was no way he could keep himself from thinking about the answer.

"A woman! It was a woman?"

Joe couldn't suppress a memory of himself and Phillip together in the firelight. He tried to cover it up with a memory of their test of unarmed combat.

Lord Elsen shook him hard. "Were you lovers or enemies? It's not clear! Tell me!"

In spite of the pain, Joe let out a gurgle of laughter. "Beats me. I couldn't figure that one out, either."

Lord Elsen swore. In a few seconds, Joe convulsed in pain. It continued for more than a minute, and then finally, everything went black again,

Eight: The Price

The next day was a blur of pain. Periodically, Lord Elsen would stop the caravan to question Joe, inflicting mental torture on top of the physical pain he suffered from his confinement.

Joe kept silent, but still Lord Elsen learned from the images that formed in Joe's mind when the dark lord asked him questions. Lord Elsen learned that Phillip was a woman posing as a man, that she seemed able to withstand magic, that she and Joe had quarreled often but made love only once, and that she had been a soldier in Lord Marcellin's guard.

Late in the afternoon, Lord Elsen called a halt to make camp. Once the prison frame was unhooked from the horse and propped up to a near-vertical position, he strolled over and spoke to Joe. "You look a mess, my friend. I doubt your androgynous lover would want you now."

Joe didn't bother to agree. He had been bound for more than a day now, and at some time during the night he had given up control of his bladder. That and the sweat, dust, and blood that covered him made for an unattractive picture.

"Well, no matter," Lord Elsen said. "At this rate you'll be dead soon."

Joe didn't answer.

"The old man didn't tell you who this woman was, did he?" Lord Elsen asked.

Lord Elsen's tone implied that he knew more about Phillip than Joe did. Even numb with pain, Joe distrusted Lord Elsen too much to speak.

"We mages have to be careful." Lord Elsen's manner grew confiding, almost chatty. "Our power depends on magic, and thus we're vulnerable to anyone whose ability is greater than our own. We take care not to allow a child who possesses innate magic to grow up. Tolliver was always too squeamish to follow good sense. I expect he settled

63

for ensorcelling the girl, to limit her magic and distract her from her potential."

Joe wavered. Speaking could be dangerous, but on the other hand, it was hard to learn anything if he kept silent. "What's innate magic?" he croaked.

Lord Elsen lifted his brows in mock surprise at the sound of Joe's voice. "Alack, poor fellow! How terrible you sound! Let me get you some water." He held a small water bottle to Joe's lips.

Joe drank greedily until Lord Elsen moved the bottle away.

"More later," he said, "if you're good."

"What's innate magic?" Joe repeated, licking his lips.

"It's an ability some people have in them," Lord Elsen said. "Some have more than others, but most people have none at all."

"So all mages have it?"

"Certainly. If you have enough innate magic, you can learn almost any spell or enchantment and make it work. If you don't have innate magic, no spell will work for you. That's how magic is, you see?"

Joe was having difficulty keeping it all straight in his head, but he could dimly recall the dragon saying that Phillip had magic in her. He also remembered the Great Mage saying something about Phillip being familiar in some way.

Lord Elsen was watching Joe's face. "I see you're beginning to fit the pieces together. You see how Tolliver could have enchanted the girl to get her out of his way. It was unlucky for him that she showed up again, but then he sent her off with you on your ridiculous quest."

"I don't believe it." As soon as he said it, Joe knew he shouldn't have spoken.

Lord Elsen smiled triumphantly. "Not yet, perhaps, but you will soon." He reached out and gently stroked Joe's forehead, leaving a cold chill everywhere he touched, a chill that numbed the pain. "If I let you live, it'll be because I have a use for you. Tools can be shaped to a purpose."

"You bloody bastard!" Joe wanted to tug at his bonds, but he had no strength.

"Tut, tut!" Lord Elsen said, clicking his tongue. "You'll have to learn more respect for your new master."

He laid his hand on Joe's head again, but instead of coldness, a sudden stabbing pain invaded Joe's brain.

Joe screamed so loudly he almost didn't hear the shout from the other side of the caravan. When the pain ceased abruptly Joe raised his head to see Lord Elsen frowning. The dark lord was staring over Joe's left shoulder.

One of the soldiers shouted again, and then several of them began running to the horses.

"Dragon!" someone screamed. "A dragon is coming!"

Panic broke out instantly. Officers shouted orders, but every man there had only one thought, and that was to reach a horse as quickly as possible. Fights broke out as soldiers struggled for mounts. Joe saw a man who had grabbed a horse's reins stabbed by another man, who vaulted onto the animal's back, only to be dragged off by a third man.

Joe craned his neck to scan the sky and finally saw a dark shape that looked black against the blue sky. The shape grew larger every second, and soon Joe could distinguish the wings that beat the air at a terrific speed. The animal flew with its long, snake-like body stretched out.

Lord Elsen had gathered a half dozen men and prepared to make a stand. Most of the men formed a circle around him and drew their swords. The two with bows each nocked an arrow.

As the dragon drew nearer, it dropped closer to the earth. Men screamed as it flew overhead, its long tail whipping back and forth, knocking riders from their horses. The dragon rose high into the air, and turned back to swoop over the camp. This time it plucked a man from his horse, grasping him with its forearms and carrying him, screaming, into the air.

When it reached a height of a few hundred feet, the dragon opened its claws. The man fell like a stone and hit the earth with a sickening thud.

No one went to his aid, as the dragon was already returning. It flew in a meandering route, swooping over terrified men and animals as if it were herding them. It belched a long, straight flame that licked the earth and scorched everything it touched. Men screamed in terror, and horses neighed and plunged as they caught the scent of burning grass and flesh.

The men around Lord Elsen held their places. And then the dragon swooped down straight at Lord Elsen and his men and belched a huge tongue of fire.

The flames didn't reach them. Lord Elsen raised his arms, and the fire turned back, as if there were a barrier between the men and the dragon.

The dragon circled and tried again, but again Lord Elsen's magic was stronger than the flames. The men in the circle cheered, and one of the archers shot an arrow at the dragon.

The men cheered louder still, even though the arrow fell short. They started to move from their circle, but Lord Elsen called them back. In just a minute, the dragon turned and came at them.

This time the dragon swooped so low it was barely above the ground. The movement of its wings caused a terrific wind that battered Joe. Dust swirled. Joe could barely see, as the dragon's tail brushed over the men's heads. The dragon turned in a tight circle and charged through the dust. Its wedge-shaped head felled two of the men, and then its tail whipped past and knocked down three others, including the dark lord.

The dragon seized its chance, twisting in mid-air to shoot down a tongue of fire that caught the men on the ground. The soldiers screamed as their clothes caught fire, and even Lord Elsen cried out. The dragon hovered, beating the air with its wings and fanning the flames. Men ran screaming, and then dropped to roll on the ground trying to put out the flames.

The dragon rose higher in the air. Lord Elsen was left alone. The flames on his clothes flickered and went out as he re-established control of his magic. He staggered away from the swirling dust and smoke. Joe could barely see him. And then a figure loomed in front of Joe's frame. For a second he thought it was one of the soldiers, and then he recognized Phillip.

"Phil!" he shouted.

"Shut up," she said, reaching up to slice the rope that bound his right wrist.

Joe's right arm dropped limply to his side. Phillip bent down and cut the ropes on his ankles, and suddenly Joe hung with all his weight on his left wrist. "Agh!"

Phillip tucked her shoulder under his left arm and cut the last rope. Joe almost fell, but she held him up. They staggered a few steps together.

"No," Joe said. "I'll never make it. You go."

"Don't be stupid," Phillip said. "I came here just to get you."

"But the dragon might come back!"

"I expect he will," she said grimly. "I haven't paid him yet."

"What?"

"Come on!" she said. "Let's get out of here before the smoke clears."

Joe couldn't walk. Even with Phillip dragging him, their progress was slow.

"Damn, I'll have to catch a horse." Phillip glanced around.

"What's that over there?" Joe asked, as a dark pillar of smoke seemed to swirl and grow solid.

Phillip took one look at it and let go of Joe, who promptly fell to the ground in a heap. "Wait here," she said.

"Phil!" Joe pulled himself into a sitting position.

She kept walking toward the dark shape. In a second, the shape moved closer, and Joe could see that it was Lord Elsen.

"So," Lord Elsen said, "it seems that you were lovers after all?"

"Pig!" Phillip said. "What did you do to him?"

Lord Elsen held out his arms in an expansive gesture. "He was reluctant to speak of you, so I had to be persuasive."

"Me?" Phillip sounded surprised.

"Of course, you," Lord Elsen said. "You have a talent that has value. I could certainly use someone with your abilities."

Phillip laughed and drew her sword. "The best thing I could do for this world would be to send you out of it."

Lord Elsen bowed as if he had just been introduced to a lady. "If you think you can, you're welcome to try." He held out his right hand, and a fallen soldier's sword flew up from the ground and into his grip.

Phillip snickered. "Parlor tricks! I expected better."

Lord Elsen shrugged. "I should hate to disappoint you." He held out his empty left hand, palm up, and in a few seconds, Phillip gasped and almost dropped her sword.

From the way she cringed, Joe knew that Lord Elsen had made the pommel too hot to hold.

"Phil!" he called. "Phil, he says you can do magic, too! I don't know what to tell you, but if you can figure out a way to do it, try!"

Phillip didn't take her eyes from Lord Elsen, but she nodded. "I will." She clutched her necklace in her left hand and resolutely gripped her sword with her right. Lord Elsen frowned and grasped his own sword more firmly.

"Die, you bastard!" Phillip suddenly yelled, and then she charged him with her sword raised to strike.

Lord Elsen easily side-stepped her charge, but he looked surprised that she had made it. He turned, always facing her as she danced about looking for a weakness in his guard.

She didn't find one, but she had help. Behind the dark lord a huge, sinuous form rose up, and a flame shot out over his head.

Lord Elsen pivoted in alarm and raised his arms as the dragon reared up behind him.

"He's mine!" Phillip screamed, and she ran Lord Elsen through where he stood, plunging her sword into his side and then quickly wrenching it free.

Lord Elsen poised on his toes, like a dancer, for a moment and then fell like cut timber.

The dragon blinked, coughed, and looked down at the body twitching on the ground. "Certainly. I wasn't trying to poach. Just checking on how things were going."

It was the old dragon from the cave. He had the same nicks and scars on his now-folded wings, but his eyes had a glitter that hadn't been there before.

Joe dragged himself over to where Lord Elsen lay and checked the body. "He's dead. Thanks, Phil."

She stood, sword in hand, her chest pumping air, and nodded. "We're even now."

Joe looked up at her in surprise. "Is that why you came back for me? Because I saved you before?"

She hesitated and then shrugged nonchalantly. "Why else?"

"Ahem," the dragon interjected diplomatically. "I don't mean to be pushy, but the soldiers that aren't dead have run off. I've done my part, and now there's the matter of my fee."

"What fee?" Joe said.

"The fee we agreed upon." The dragon's mental tone was firm. "Are you ready, my dear?"

Phillip looked suddenly pale. She stood stock still and said nothing.

"You did agree," the dragon pointed out. "You gave your word."

She let her sword fall, sucked in a deep breath, and let it out with a shudder. "I'm ready."

"Phil?" Joe said in alarm. "What did you promise?"

"Open your shirt, just a little," the dragon instructed. "And then hold perfectly still."

"Phil!" Joe shouted, remembering the woman who had been eaten. "What's going on?"

Wordlessly, Phillip pulled her shirt open. Joe watched in alarm as the dragon slithered over to her, raising small clouds of dust.

"Damn it!" Joe shouted, enraged at his own helpless state. "You hurt her, you bloody lizard, and I'll chop you into sushi!"

"Be quiet," the dragon answered tartly. "You're distracting me."

He extended his neck and held his head exactly in front of Phillip's face. His long forked tongue flicked out and wrapped around her neck for a second, as if he were gauging the distance. "Don't move!"

Phillip didn't move, but her face and bosom were very pale.

Suddenly, the stone on her necklace began to glow.

"Ahh!" The dragon was plainly pleased. "Lovely!" His tongue flicked out and caught the chain, twining around the links. The dragon turned his head sideways as if he planned to kiss Phillip on her neck. She tilted her head, and suddenly the dragon jerked his head backwards with a lightning fast snap.

Phillip cried out as if she were in pain, and in the same instant, the chain of her necklace broke with a sharp crack.

The dragon tossed his head back and let the necklace drop into his mouth. He swallowed in one gulp, and then lowered his head and smiled at Phillip. "Thank you so much, my dear. You have no idea what this means to me."

And with that, he slithered away a few dozen yards, moving at an incredible speed, and then flapped his wings and launched himself into the air.

Joe swore with relief. "I was afraid he was going to eat you."

Phillip stood motionless and silent.

Joe grew alarmed. "Phil? You okay?"

She didn't answer. Joe had started to drag himself closer when she closed her eyes and sank to the ground in a dead faint.

$\mathcal{N}$INE: THE RETURN

Joe searched the soldiers' discarded gear and found blankets, clothes, and supplies, including food and water. He made a rude tent—the best he could do with limited mobility—and was glad of it when it rained during the night. He slept next to the still-unconscious Phillip to keep them both warm.

In the morning, Joe crawled out from the shelter and surveyed the carnage. Between huge patches of scorched earth, bodies lay scattered about under the clear blue sky. Joe had dragged Phillip as far away from the dead as he could, in case there were scavengers, but none of the bodies showed signs of having been disturbed.

In the distance, a horse grazed. Joe stumbled toward it, hoping to persuade it to let him get near before it ran off. The horse never moved, and when Joe got closer he saw that the still-saddled gelding had caught his reins in the roots of a bush. The horse skittered when the man got close. Joe clucked soothingly and spoke softly. Once the animal was still, Joe stroked its neck before he untangled the reins.

He led the horse back to the shelter and found Phillip standing there watching him.

"Hello," Joe said. "How are you? I was worried about you."

She didn't speak but only stared at him with wide, frightened eyes.

"Come on," Joe said, hoping a firm tone would help. "Time to head back."

She didn't answer, but she followed his directions and helped him collect supplies and his pack, which had providentially been abandoned, and still contained the seven dragon scales.

It was while they were assembling their supplies that Joe first noticed the strange shape in the sky. He thought at first that it was the dragon coming back, but as it got closer, the shape didn't look right. It was too wide, and its path was erratic, traversing the sky in wide loops and swoops.

71

When it was almost overhead, Joe realized it was two dragons, their bodies twined together in an incredible aerial ballet—a winged double helix. They never lost touch as they flew over the plain, but they were constantly in motion—an unceasing undulation of serpentine bodies moving together, their wings beating the air with rhythmic precision.

The spectacle passed quickly, moving out of sight in a matter of seconds, but Joe was quite certain that one of the two was the old dragon from the cave.

"It looks like you did the old guy a real favor," he said to Phillip.

She said nothing, but stared at the spot in the sky where the dragons had last been visible.

Joe went back to deciding what they should carry with them. He couldn't find their map, but he figured if they headed east, they were bound to hit the Great Barrier—unless they were already too far north, in which case they might encounter Lord Elsen's soldiers, out searching for their mage.

Joe knew it would tire the horse to carry two riders, but he didn't feel up to walking. He mounted and then directed Phillip to get up behind him, leaning down to offer her a hand. She pulled herself up without a word.

He tried talking to Phil, but she never responded. When he reached back to pat her knee reassuringly, she pulled away from him, so Joe didn't repeat the gesture.

They rested part-way through the morning, and then Joe walked for a few miles, to stretch his legs. He had Phillip mount the horse, and then he held the reins while she sat dumbly in the saddle and let him lead. It was so unlike her that Joe was further alarmed.

After a while, walking didn't hurt so much. When they stopped to eat at noon, he had to suggest delicately to Phillip that she should relieve herself. She looked confused but she did wander off alone for a few minutes.

When they made camp at night, Joe did most of the work, as Phillip sat quietly unless directed otherwise. She ate what he gave her, but with no sign of enjoyment, and lay down on her bed roll when he told her to.

Sometime in the night, Joe woke to find Phillip clutching him in her sleep. She wept quietly, but with her eyes closed. Joe held her close, in spite of the pain it caused his burned chest.

In the morning Phil seemed more alert. She looked around more, and didn't have to be told to see to her body's needs. When Joe had her mount the horse and then took the reins, she leaned over the saddle horn and held out her hand. "You don't need to lead."

It was the first time she had spoken since the dragon had eaten her necklace. Joe let her hold the reins, and after they stopped to rest in a few hours, he let her walk for a ways while he rode the horse.

It was shortly after they had switched places again that they saw the line of mounted soldiers in the distance. There were forty of them, and Joe was torn as to whether to try to elude them or not.

"It's all right," Phillip said in flat tones. "They won't hurt us."

Joe decided to trust her instinct or her magic, whichever it was. He mounted the horse behind her, and she clucked to the animal to move forward. In a few minutes the soldiers changed direction and headed straight for Phillip and Joe on their lone horse.

As soon as they were close, Joe breathed a sigh of relief. The soldiers wore the Great Mage's livery.

The officer at their head, one of Joe's former students, reined in his troop as they drew close. "Ho, good sir! You leave on foot and return on a horse! It must have been a successful quest."

"Yes," Joe said. "We're glad to see you, Gilbert. Were you looking for us?"

Gilbert grinned widely. "Indeed. The Great Mage informed us that you'd most likely return from this direction."

Gilbert had brought two extra horses. Joe rode one and Phillip the other, as their own steed was in need of a rest.

Joe rode beside Gilbert and informed him that Lord Elsen was dead.

Gilbert nodded sagely. "We knew something was afoot. There have been wild rumors. There's always chaos for a while after a dark lord dies."

"What will happen in Lord Elsen's ward? Who will rule it?"

"Only time can answer that," Gilbert said. "Anyone in the valley who has magic in him and aspires to be a mage will make his way there. If there's more than one, they may battle each other."

"You mean with magic?"

"Yes, and with soldiers." Gilbert seemed sanguine about the future, but perhaps he felt no one could be worse than Lord Elsen. "It's also possible that Lord Marcellin could try to assume Lord Elsen's ward in addition to his own, but it's not likely. Lord Marcellin isn't a strong enough mage to hold that much land."

There seemed another possibility to Joe. "Do you think the Great Mage would try to take over Lord Elsen's ward, too?"

"I doubt it," Gilbert said. "He has said that he made the barrier as big as he could make it, and even that didn't take in all the land he claims as his ward. I don't think he'd stretch himself further."

Joe considered this statement, but Gilbert interrupted his thoughts.

"So it's true your companion is a woman? I'd heard the rumor, but when I saw her before, I didn't believe it."

Joe glanced back at Phillip, riding silently a little ways behind them. He had to agree that she looked subtly different. The more womanly curves of her figure were easily explained, as she hadn't made any attempt to bind her breasts since the dragon had eaten her necklace. But somehow her features seemed softer and less angular, and she had done nothing to change her face.

"Oh, she's a woman all right," he said.

Gilbert gave him a curious look but said no more.

Joe fell to anticipating the pleasure of a hot bath waiting for him back at the Barrier fort. When he expressed this sentiment out loud, Gilbert laughed.

"I didn't want to be rude, but you do look a sight. You must have had a rough time of it."

Joe grinned. "You should have seen me—and smelled me—before I found a change of clothes this morning." He went on to tell Gilbert about the battle. Gilbert expressed the opinion that they had been fortunate in their choice of an ally.

"That was Phil's doing," Joe said. "But it was a good choice. Once the dragon flew overhead, they all took off running."

"After all," Gilbert said, "would you care to face an angry dragon—or a hungry one?"

"No," Joe said. "I was damn glad to hear the dragon was on our side."

They reached the barrier a little before dark, and Joe was gratified to be once more in the Great Mage's ward, and inside the barrier.

ω

They left the barrier fort at dawn, on the Great Mage's orders. Joe hadn't argued. He was anxious to get back to the palace himself, as he had some questions for the Great Mage.

Phillip didn't seem in a hurry, but she didn't protest their departure. She didn't speak much on the journey, but she did answer when Joe asked her questions.

"Say, Phil," Joe said, directing his horse nearer to hers, "have you thought anymore about what you're going to do when the Great Mage releases you?"

She gave him a brief, inscrutable glance and looked away. "A little."

"So did you decide anything?"

"No."

And that was all she would say on that subject.

"Did I remember to thank you for saving my life?" Joe asked, trying another tack.

"Yes."

"It was pretty smart of you to go back to the dragon for help. How did you get there?"

She gave him another peculiar look. "I ran most of the way."

"But how did you get there from the river?"

She shrugged indifferently. "I was never in the river. I jumped down to a ledge on the near bank, threw a rock in the water to make a splash, and hid under the bushes until the soldiers gave up searching. Then I went back the way we had come, but faster."

"You made good time," Joe said.

"I was in a hurry. And once I'd found him, the dragon carried me when he flew. It took us a while to find the caravan, but I knew they'd head north, and dragons can fly very fast."

"You rode on a dragon's back?" Joe said, amazed. "Wow!"

"What does 'wow' mean?" she said, sounding cross.

"Oh, sorry. Wow is an exclamation—like saying 'how extraordinary.' "

"Oh."

"Really, Phil, I'd have been terrified. Weren't you scared at all?"

She hesitated. "A little," she said at last.

Joe shook his head admiringly. "You're a damn fine soldier, Phil. You've got brains and guts, and you don't give up."

"Thank you." Somehow she sounded as if she didn't take it as a compliment. Without speaking another word, she nudged her horse forward and left Joe riding by himself.

"Oh, yeah," Joe muttered to himself. "She's a woman all right. Boy, I sure can pick 'em."

TEN: THE DECISION

As soon they rode into the courtyard, Joe saw Mother Wilhelmina standing on the steps of the main hall. She gave first him and then Phillip an anxious once-over glance.

"Good afternoon, Joseph," she said as he dismounted. "It's good to see you."

"Thank you, Mother." Joe stooped to give her a brief embrace and flinched as his burn pained him.

She looked dismayed and beckoned the sister who waited behind her. "Joseph has injuries. Take him to the infirmary and see to them."

"Yes, Mother." The woman stepped aside for Joe to precede her.

"But what about Phillip?" Joe asked. "I want to be there when she sees the Great Mage."

Mother Wilhelmina gave Phillip a quick glance but shook her head. "The Great Mage has directed that he'll see Phillip alone."

Joe tried to argue, but Mother Wilhelmina reminded of his oath of obedience, and Joe was borne off by the waiting sisters. He was a little embarrassed to be tended by the sisters again. When he first came to the Great Mage's ward, he had been too ill to be embarrassed at being seen naked by a series of strange women. Now he wasn't sick, and he knew several of the sisters rather well. They weren't a religious order but merely a group of women who dedicated their lives to caring for the sick. Joe had found the ones near his own age to be good company, and willing to indulge in occasional intimacy. They had made life in the Great Mage's ward tolerable.

Sister Zenobiya was old enough to be his mother, and indeed, he had never seen her as anything but a maternal sort of friend. The sister who held the basin was another story, and Joe avoided meeting her eye. He had to lie naked on a bed while Sister Zenobiya examined him and then washed the cuts and contusions that covered his body. She slathered the knife-shaped burn with a soothing ointment, and Joe hoped his ordeal would soon be over.

And then Mother Wilhelmina came into the room.

"And how is Joseph?" Mother Wilhelmina asked as Joe snatched at the sheets and clutched them around his genitals.

"He'll be fine, Mother," Sister Zenobiya said. "His only serious injury is a burn. We'll watch it to be sure it heals without infection."

Mother Wilhelmina scrutinized the burn and agreed with her prognosis. "You may dress now, Joseph. The Great Mage will see you in his laboratory."

"Where's Phil?" Joe asked.

"I believe she's resting," Mother Wilhelmina thanked the sisters, and directed them to leave with her so that Joe could dress alone.

Joe took his time. Eager as he was to see the Great Mage, the laboratory was his least favorite place. He climbed the stairs alone, and knocked on the door with trepidation.

"Come," a voice called.

Joe opened the door.

The Great Mage sat at the desk, writing in a large book. He wrote one last word, and looked up. "Come in, friend Joe!"

Joe advanced cautiously. The laboratory was small, almost a perfect square, with a desk and stool on one side and a long bench and laboratory table on the other. Light came in from several skylights above them.

The Great Mage closed his book. "Something tells me you have questions for me."

"Yes, sir," Joe said, suddenly unsure how to begin.

"I know how your quest fared," the Great Mage said, "and I know Lord Elsen is dead. What do you need to know from me?"

"Who is Phil?" Joe blurted out. "Lord Elsen and the dragon both said she had innate magic."

Amusement lurked in the Great Mage's eyes. "That's true enough."

"Did you know that before you sent us on the quest?"

"Certainly, I knew."

"But who is she, sir? You said you thought you knew her."

The mage's amusement faded to concern. "I found her when she was five years old."

"Found her?"

The mage nodded. "Once a year I search the countryside to see if there are children with innate magic. I found Phillip, as she calls herself now, on her family's farm. It was outside the barrier—" The Great Mage broke off abruptly and frowned. "What dark thoughts are these? Who's been poisoning your mind against me?"

Joe flushed but didn't speak.

"Well?" the mage insisted. "Why do you find my actions reprehensible?"

"I don't—it's just—Lord Elsen said that all mages search out anyone in their wards who has innate magic and—and destroy them."

The Great Mage rose to his feet, and somehow seemed to tower over Joe. "And you believed I destroy talented children?"

"No, sir." He hadn't really believed it, but once introduced, the thought had been difficult to expunge. "Then Lord Elsen said—he suggested you put a spell on Phil to make her want to be a man so she couldn't concentrate on her magic."

The mage slipped his hands into his sleeves and frowned. "How long did Lord Elsen have you in his power?"

"Less than two days," Joe said. "Why, sir?"

"Because a mage of Lord Elsen's power, with no compunction about using people—and I assure you he had none—could easily consume the mind of someone with no innate magic."

Joe remembered the touch of Lord Elsen's hand on his forehead—ice cold, remorseless, and yet numbing the pain. "I think he planned to do that."

The Great Mage held out his hands. "Tell me again what he said."

Joe walked forward resolutely and let the mage lay his hands on his shoulders.

"Now," the Great Mage ordered, "close your eyes and think back! Remember what he did to you and what he said."

Joe obeyed, and in a moment he felt sharp fear as he recalled seeing Lord Elsen's soldiers, his pain on waking, the hours of torture and suffering until Phillip had come. And then, somehow, the memory no longer had the power to hurt him or frighten him.

"Now," the Great Mage said, letting go of him, "I'll tell you about Phillip."

Joe opened his eyes and waited.

"As I said," the mage went on, "I found her when she was five. Her family had a farm southeast of here, outside the Great Barrier. In my arrogance, I thought I could keep her—Estrella her name was when she was small—I thought I could keep Estrella safe by keeping her existence a secret. When she was eight, I found out how wrong I was. She was stolen from her family, and I never saw her until the day you took me to the infirmary."

"But," Joe said, perplexed, "who took her and why?"

"Ah!" the Great Mage said. "The who is supposition, but I think it must have been Lady Merida. She has the cleverness to have come up with the ensorcellment that Phillip suffered."

"The necklace?"

"That was the clever part," the Great Mage said. "The necklace was merely a focus for the spell; the power behind it came from Estrella's innate magic. So long as she wore the necklace, Estrella wanted to be male—to be Phillip. It was her own magic that made her appear masculine, and the older she got, the more her magic grew, and the stronger the spell became. The strength of her talent made the chain unbreakable. It seemed safest to find a way to remove it."

"How do you mean?"

"Well," the mage said, "I needed to make Estrella want not to be male. I reasoned that if she fell in love with a man, she'd want to be a woman."

"So you sent her to fetch dragon scales to make a love potion?"

The mage nodded. "That was the plan, but as it turned out, the potion was unnecessary."

Joe said nothing.

The Great Mage went on. "Remember Estrella has always had her own magic. As soon as she saw you, her magic told her you were someone she could love. That was why she screamed and shouted abuse at you. And at some point, out there on your quest, she fell in love with you on her own, with no help from me."

Joe remembered the night he and Phillip had made love and blushed.

The Great Mage smiled and nodded. "Once she loved you, Estrella could resist the spell by touching you."

"Are you saying she's still in love with me?" Joe said slowly.

"Oh, yes. Why do you think she worked so hard to rescue you? And when the dragon refused to help unless she gave him the one object she wanted most to keep, she agreed to give it up to save you."

"But," Joe said, "the necklace is gone now, and she hardly spoke to me all the way here."

The Great Mage shook his head in mock despair. "Joe, Joe, my friend! The poor girl has no idea how to act like a woman. All she knows is how to be a man and a soldier. She doesn't even know how to ask you if you care for her."

Joe thought this over. "Where do you come into this, sir? I mean, what's your interest in Phil?"

"Ah! I was waiting for you to come to that point. I don't intend to let my ward fall into chaos and despair after my death. Estrella will take my place and rule after me."

"Is that why Lady Merida stole her away?"

"Perhaps. Merida is younger than I, and she might have hoped to seize this ward if I died with no heir ready to assume my place."

"Why didn't Lady Merida simply kill Phil? Why keep her alive?"

"Who can say?" the Great Mage said, "Merida may have thought an untrained mage of Estrella's power could be of use."

"What did Phil say when you told her this?" Joe asked.

The Great Mage smiled reflectively. "More than anything else, she was stunned to find that she has a family. Her parents are alive, and she has brothers and sisters. I plan to fetch her family here tomorrow.

I don't want her going outside the barrier again until she's learned how to use her magic to protect herself."

"That makes sense," Joe said. "And I'm glad she has a family. She was lonely growing up."

"She was indeed."

"So," Joe said, "is she willing to be your heir?"

"She hasn't decided. She's intrigued by power but afraid of it. I'm more worried about how she'll do as a mage."

"I thought you said she had lots of innate magic?"

"She does, she does. But having magic to spare is no guarantee you'll be a just mage. I had intended to keep Estrella by my side as she grew, so that she might learn what's involved in ruling people without letting the power go to your head."

Joe recalled Lord Elsen and nodded. "So what will you do about Phi—Estrella now?"

The Great Mage walked over to the table where a row of bottles and implements stood on a shelf. An iridescent sheen gleamed on the table top. "Come here, please, Joe."

Joe followed the mage reluctantly. He had never cared for proximity to the paraphernalia of magic. In his heart of hearts, he feared it.

The mage waited for Joe to approach, and then he opened a wooden casket on the table. Inside lay a glass bottle, securely stoppered with a cork. "This is a love potion," the Great Mage said. "I had intended to make it for Estrella, so that she'd fall in love with you, but since that wasn't needed, I made it for you, so that you'll fall in love with her. I think it would be best if you drink it now."

"What?" Joe asked, sure he couldn't have heard the Great Mage correctly.

"I created this potion with a spell that will make you fall in love with Estrella," the mage said. "After you drink it, you won't be able to stop yourself from loving her."

"You expect me to drink that," Joe said incredulously, "after what you just told me?"

"Precisely," the mage said. "She needs you."

"Needs me? For what?"

"To be a good mage. To be a benevolent despot instead of a dark lady." The Mage shook his head despairingly. "The people who took Estrella in wanted a servant, not a child. No one taught her ethics or fairness. No one taught her to consider the suffering of others as her own."

Joe remembered how Phil had planned to leave the raiders' bodies on the trail. "You can still teach her."

"I could if she cared for my opinion like she cares for yours. If she sees disgust or revulsion in your eyes, she'll care a great deal. And you have all those qualities, my friend. You could serve as Estrella's conscience."

"Jimminy Cricket," Joe said.

"What?" the mage asked.

"Nothing. It's irrelevant."

The mage pushed the glass bottle across the table top and waited.

Joe stared at him and didn't move.

"It depends," the mage said clearly, "on how you feel about Estrella. If you think you care about her—if you think you could love her— you'll drink the potion. If what happened between you two meant no more to you than the pleasant interludes you enjoyed with some of the sisters, then you won't drink it. You will let her love you, but you won't try to love her back."

Joe stood frozen, staring at the glass bottle on the table. It was a small bottle, holding no more than half a cup of liquid. The potion itself was almost the color of honey, but with a swirl of sparkling colors deep in its center.

Joe remembered the first time he had seen Phillip as she fought so fiercely, struggling to stay on her feet after she was wounded. He remembered her courage when the outlaws had held her down on the boulder and cut her clothes off her. He remembered her looming up out of the dust, coming straight to him to slice through his bonds.

And then suddenly all Joe could think of was how Phil had felt in his arms that one night they had been lovers—how she had delighted in his touch and in touching him back. Before he could change his mind, Joe uncorked the bottle and drained it in one long gulping swallow.

"Agh!" he gasped. "That stuff is too damn sweet!"

The Great Mage smiled. "Love is sweet."

Joe took a deep breath and waited expectantly. "What happens now?"

"To you, you mean?" The mage put the cork back in the bottle. "Nothing until you see Estrella. Then you'll be overcome by tender feelings. Even if a path to your world opened on your doorstep, you wouldn't go through it because you'd want to stay with her."

"Is that likely to happen?" Joe asked in surprise. "A path opening to my world?"

"Not to my knowledge." The mage put the empty bottle back into the casket. "But stranger things have happened."

Stranger things than Joe had ever dreamed of back in Glencoe, Illinois. "I suppose so."

"You had better go now," the mage said gently. "Estrella is waiting. I sent her to your room to wait for you."

"Yes," Joe said, suddenly confused. He wanted very much to see her, but he was afraid. "I suppose I'd better go."

The Great Mage nodded toward the door, and Joe turned to leave.

"Good luck, Joseph," the mage said as Joe put his hand on the door. "And thank you."

"You don't need to thank me, sir," Joe said over his shoulder. "But I can use the luck. She's not an easy person to be in love with."

The Great Mage laughed at this. "Do you know someone who is?"

"I don't know." Joe had never thought about it that way. "I suppose love is never easy."

"It will be for you," the mage said. "Go now, Joe."

ω

Joe stood outside his door and debated whether to knock. It was his room, but the woman on the other side of the door might expect privacy.

Finally, the door was ripped open. "Are you coming in or not?" Phillip demanded.

"Yes," Joe said, annoyed at being challenged on his own doorstep. "I'm coming in."

He strode inside and shut the door. When he turned and saw Phillip, she looked very different from the last time he had seen her in this room.

Her hair was very slightly longer, but that wasn't it. She still wore trousers, but her shirt looked more like a woman's blouse. Open at the throat, it made her neck look swan-like. Her slenderness made her elegant rather than boyish.

"Did those women help you?" Phillip said.

"They put something on the burn," Joe said. "It'll be okay."

"Good." She looked down at the floor as if she had run out of things to say.

"Phil," Joe began, "I mean, Estrella—"

"Don't call me that," she said. "Call me Phil like you always do."

"Okay, Phil. I wanted to ask you—I mean, I wanted to tell you—"

"It's all right," she said, turning away from him. "I know what you're trying to say."

"You do?" he said in surprise.

"Yes," she said, still with her back to him. "I know you've had—lovers. I know which of the sisters have been in your bed. You want a woman who looks like a woman—who acts like a woman. You don't want someone like me."

"That's not true!" Joe blurted out. She turned swiftly, and he felt compelled to be honest. "I mean, yes, I've had lovers, but I do want you, Phil. I love you."

He knew, as soon as he said it, that it was true. The Great Mage's potion had worked swiftly. The thought of leaving her, or of her leaving him, left him with a wrenching emptiness.

Phillip stood poised, waiting, as if she expected a sign from him. Joe held out his arms, and she stepped into them.

"Oh, Joe, Joe, I was so afraid you wouldn't want me!"

"Don't be silly, Phil."

She pushed him away as if she felt a need to look at his face when she spoke. "I can't be a frilly woman. I won't wear dresses. I won't wear my hair long, or flirt, or be weak and helpless. I was a man too long to be like that."

"I don't need frills or long hair. And you don't have to be weak to be a woman. You just have to love me and want me."

Her eyes told him all that he ever needed to know. He pulled her close again and kissed her. Somehow—he wasn't quite certain how—they ended up falling over onto his bed.

ω

A little while later, Joe propped himself up on one elbow. "It's never been like that before," he said, breathless and a little surprised. "And you're definitely a woman, Phil."

She smiled warmly and stroked his cheek. "I think I'll change my name to Phyllida. That way no one will think it strange when you call me Phil."

He smiled back and kissed her.

She gave a little sigh of contentment and nestled against him. "I hope being a mage is as much fun as being a woman."

"It had better not be," Joe said.

"Now tell me!" Phyllida ordered, "What did you mean when you said you'd chop the dragon into sushi?"

*E*PILOGUE: *T*HE *T*RUTH

Mother Wilhelmina knocked at the door of the laboratory.

"Come," called a voice.

She opened the door and saw the Great Mage at his desk. He didn't look up when she walked in. Mother Wilhelmina leaned over and kissed the bald spot on the top of his head.

He smiled up at her. "Hello, Willie."

She kissed him on the mouth and patted his shoulder. "How did it go?"

"Fine," the mage said. "He drank the potion willingly. I didn't need to use undue persuasion."

"So now he'll stay with her always?"

"Yes," the mage said, giving her a fond smile. "He can serve as her conscience, just as you've been mine since I found you."

She looked over at the table and clucked in concern. "You're always so untidy with your spells, Tolliver."

She went over to the table and began to clear away the implements he had left out. When she opened a drawer to replace the mortar and pestle, she gasped in surprise. In a large, flat box, seven iridescent dragon scales twinkled in the dim light. "Tolliver! Did you give that young man a love potion or did you not?"

The Great Mage came close and looked over her shoulder. He moved one of the scales, and she saw that a third of it was gone. "I did, but only a very mild one. It wouldn't have done anything if he hadn't been half in love with the girl already."

Mother Wilhelmina gave a snort of annoyance. "You and your clever tricks! Why did you bother if you weren't going to give him a full-strength potion?"

"Two reasons," the Great Mage said, "I wanted him to think he was hopelessly and completely in love with Estrella, but I didn't want to tell him an outright lie. He soon will be in love with her, and having

taken even a mild potion, he'll enjoy the physical side of their relation-
ship much more, and never be tempted to stray."

Mother Wilhelmina shook her head.   This situation was too
convoluted for her way of thinking. "And what was the other reason?"

The Great Mage shut his book and put down his pen. "Some day
Estrella will ask me if I made Joe fall in love with her. I want to be able
to say that I merely gave him a nudge in the right direction."

"Will you tell him that you proposed to give him the potion secretly,
and she said not to?"

"There's no need," the Great Mage said.

"Well," Mother Wilhelmina said, "I hope the two of them will be
as happy as we've been together."

"Yes," the mage said, kissing her hand. "Your world has been very
good to mine. I'm very lucky you wandered into this valley."

Mother Wilhelmina laughed happily at this compliment. "You're
sweet, Tolliver." She glanced around the laboratory and sighed. "Now
if you could only conjure up a decent cup of coffee."